When Your Parents Pull Apart

KEEPING YOUR LIFE TOGETHER . . .

WHEN YOUR PARENTS PULL APART

Angela Elwell Hunt

AN AUTHORS GUILD BACKINPRINT.COM EDITION

Keeping Your Life Together When Your Parents Pull Apart:
A Teen's Guide To Surviving Divorce
All Rights Reserved © 1995, 2000 by Angela Elwell Hunt

AN AUTHORS GUILD BACKINPRINT.COM EDITION

Published by iUniverse.com, Inc.

For information address:
iUniverse.com, Inc.
620 North 48th Street, Suite 201
Lincoln, NE 68504-3467
www.iuniverse.com

Originally published by Tyndale House Publishers, Inc.

Scripture quotations are taken from the *Holy Bible,*
New International Version® Copyright © 1973, 1978, 1984 by International Bible Society.
Used by permission of Zondervan Publishing House. All rights reserved.
The *NIV* and *New International Version* trademarks are registered in the United States Patent and
Trademark Office by International Bible Society. Use of either trademark requires the permission of
International Bible Society.

ISBN: 0-595-08999-2

Printed in the United States of America

CONTENTS

For this reason I kneel before the Father, from whom his whole **family** in heaven and on earth derives its name. I pray that out of his **glorious riches** he may strengthen you with power through his Spirit in your inner being, so that Christ may dwell in your hearts through faith. And I pray that you, being rooted and established in love, may have power, together with all the saints, to grasp how

wide
and long
and high
and deep
is the love of Christ,

and to know this love that surpasses knowledge—that you may be filled to the measure of all the fullness of God. Now to him who is able to do immeasurably more than all **we ask or imagine,** according to his power that is at work within us, to him be glory in the church and in Christ Jesus throughout all generations, for ever and ever!
Amen.
Ephesians 3:14-21

PROLOGUE

My name is Kelsey Katherine Davis, and this is my journal, assigned by my beautiful and intelligent ninth-grade English teacher. (Hello, Miss Westgate, are you really reading this?) Anyway, I'm sitting here in English class, dreading the coming semester, mainly because the wonderful Miss Westgate made us sit in alphabetical order and I have to sit next to Kenyon, my twin brother. Everyone knows we're twins even though we don't look anything alike, but only a select few (Kenyon's friends, mostly) know that he's six minutes older than I. Those six minutes have ruined my life because Kenyon thinks he can order me around.

I've never kept a journal before, and I'm only keeping this one because Miss W. said we wouldn't pass freshman English without it. So I officially inaugurate the opening page of my journal, and I sincerely hope, Miss Westgate, that you won't feel that you have to read this entire notebook. Every page is as outstanding as this one, I promise. But when you grade Kenyon's journal, be sure to read every word. I'd bet my life the last few pages are nothing but sports scores or notes to his friends.

CHAPTER O N E

The Beginning of the End

Kenyon beat me off the school bus, and I knew I was out of luck when my history book slipped off my notebook and landed on the sidewalk. Kenyon would have a good head start and beat me home. That meant he'd blab to Mom about my detention before I had a chance to explain.

I knew Mom wouldn't like having to pick me up after school for three days, and she wouldn't understand that it was all Dorian Thompson's fault. Dorian was the one talking in Mrs. Haynes's class—I was only *listening*. But Horrible Haynes slapped both of us with a three-day detention.

By the time I picked up my history book and got moving again, Kenyon was already sprinting across our lawn. I consoled myself with the thought that if Kenyon got to Mom first, maybe he'd be so busy stuffing his face that he'd forget to tell Mom about my detention.

But when I finally made it into the kitchen, my mother was already frowning. Kenyon sat on a bar stool with half an Oreo sticking out of his mouth and a lopsided grin on his face.

I could feel my cheeks burning as Mom turned toward me. "What's this about detention?" she snapped, her hands on her hips. "Why can't my fourteen-year-old daughter learn to

1

be quiet in school? There's a time for everything, young lady, and school isn't the place for messing around."

"I wasn't messing around—," I tried to explain. I put my books on the counter and glared at Kenyon. "Dorian was talking, and I—"

"You're hanging around with the wrong people," Mom answered, cutting me off. "Tomorrow I'll have to leave here early, pick you up, and then go to work. Don't you think I have better things to do than act as your chauffeur?" Mom waved a pot holder in the air. "You can do the dishes tonight, Kelsey, and every night that you have detention."

Kenyon smirked at me behind Mom's back. I felt like throwing my history book at him, but instead I turned and ran up the stairs to my room. Slamming the door made me feel a little better.

<hr />

I called Dorian right away. She'd understand how I felt. After all, she had detention, too.

"I should have known she'd be upset," I murmured into the telephone as Dorian listened sympathetically. "My mom can't stand for anything or anybody to mess up her schedule." I sighed dramatically. "Now if I had given her two weeks' notice, it wouldn't have been such a big deal."

"At least your mom is organized," Dorian answered. "My mom is such a flake! Honestly, I've been reminding her for weeks about the western jamboree at church, and she still hasn't sewn the rhinestones on my denim shirt. By the way, Kels, what western duds have you come up with?"

I made a face. Actually, I hadn't thought much about the jamboree. I'd been thinking more about how to get Jason Smithfield to invite me on the hayride.

"I dunno," I answered. "I guess I'll just wear jeans, a shirt, and my boots."

"I know you've been thinking about Jason," Dorian said. (Sometimes it's not easy having a best friend who can read your mind!) Her voice took on a mimicking tone. "Remember, Kelsey, we don't go to church to see the guys. We go to worship the Lord."

"I worship the Lord just fine, thank you," I answered. "God and I are on great terms. I'm just trying to get on better terms with Jason."

We giggled together, then I heard Dorian take a deep breath. "Enough already," Dorian said, still laughing. "I've gotta go. See you tomorrow at school."

"Sure," I answered. "Tomorrow."

I hung up the phone and listened as a car pulled up in the driveway. The creak of a car door told me that my father was home. "Rats," I muttered to myself. "Time for round two. Dad'll start on me about detention as soon as Mom tells him."

But after ten minutes passed and Dad didn't appear, I slunk down the stairway to check out the situation. Mom and Dad stood in the hallway, and Dad was carrying a black suit encased in a dry cleaner's plastic bag. "What do you mean, you're working tonight?" Dad said, a slightly offended tone in his voice. "I told you two weeks ago about this benefit, and I was sure you put it on the calendar."

"Honestly, Dan, I don't remember anything about it," Mom answered. "And I can't do a thing about it now. Marge expects me to cover the store from five until closing tonight, and I can't ask someone else to step in at this late date. I'm sorry, but you'll just have to go without me."

Dad frowned, but he threw the suit over his shoulder and

turned toward the stairs. "Too bad, hon, you'll miss seeing me in my tux."

My mom shook her head as she turned away. "I can't say I'll be missing much," she called as she went back to the kitchen.

I looked up from where I sat on the stairs as my dad passed. "Hello, kitten," he said, patting me on the top of my head. He always does that—like I'm some kind of domestic animal. "How was school today?"

"I got detention," I mumbled.

"That's nice," Dad answered absently, and as he continued up the stairs, I was amazed to hear him whistling.

Mom left for work as she always did at 4:45 sharp, and for dinner Kenyon and I ate bowls of warmed-over spaghetti. "Too bad you've got to do the dishes all by yourself," Kenyon taunted.

"Too bad you're such a dweeb," I answered. "Too bad you're so ugly."

"Too bad you're younger than me," Kenyon shot back. "You're always too slow."

"Too bad you popped out first," I muttered. "The doctor was just practicing on you. I think he gave you brain damage."

"That's enough, you two." I turned to see Dad standing in the kitchen doorway. He was dressed in a tuxedo, and Kenyon actually whistled. I had to admit that for a forty-something-year-old man, my father was downright good-looking. His hair, still full and only slightly brushed with gray, was combed to perfection, and his dark eyes snapped with excitement.

"I'll be out late, so I'm trusting you two not to kill each

4

other before your mom comes home, OK?" Dad adjusted his cuff links and paused before the mirror to check his reflection.

"Where are you going, Dad?" Kenyon asked, forgetting his war with me. "What's the occasion?"

"It's a benefit to raise money for a center for battered women," Dad answered, brushing imaginary lint from the lapel of his tux.

"I didn't know you were into benefits," I said, crinkling my nose. "I thought you always said we gave our money for charity at the church."

Mr. Davis shrugged. "I'm not into benefits," he said. "But somebody's got to build the center, doesn't he? And won't somebody need an architect?"

He gave himself a final glance, then winked at me. "Got to go. I'm going out early to do some work with a client, so I'll see you guys tomorrow." He paused to pat Kenyon on the shoulder, then went out the door whistling again.

~~~~~~~~~~~~~

Kenyon left me to do the dishes alone, and when the kitchen was clean enough for my mother's meticulous standards, I wiped my hands on a dishtowel and tiptoed into the dining room. From Mom's china hutch, I took a cup and saucer. The hutch is full of antique china, really pretty stuff covered in a delicate green-and-yellow pattern. Mom says the china was her grandmother's and someday it will be mine, so (figure this out!) we never use it. "Family traditions," Mom always says "are terribly important. Without them, what do you have?"

I've never thought of an answer, but I've always thought it was silly to let that beautiful china just sit in the hutch. So lots of times while Mom is at work, I'll get a cup and saucer and make myself a cup of tea, or even fill a teacup with ice cubes and Coke. What's the use of having pretty things if you never use them?

I filled my teacup with diet Coke (all that Mom had on hand), balanced it on its delicate saucer, and crept to my father's office. I wasn't really supposed to be in Dad's office because when we were little Kenyon and I had ruined more than one set of Dad's blueprints and drawings. Now I knew better than to mess with the sheaf of papers rolled out on his drafting table; instead I went to his desk, put down my teacup, and wriggled into Dad's leather chair.

I love my dad's chair. Over the years the leather has assumed his shape and even his smell, and sitting in his chair reminds me of my classy dad. The chair was the first thing he bought when he was really beginning to achieve success as an architect, and even though Mom had protested that we couldn't afford a five-hundred-dollar chair, Dad had said, "You wait, Barbara. I'm going for the best, and I'll have it all. This chair will remind me of that every time I sit down."

He had kept his word, and now all around the office I could see the trappings of my dad's success. There were plaques on the wall announcing awards for design and skill, expensive knickknacks on his bookshelves, and art books by the score that he hardly ever opened. A sleek fax machine sat on the far corner of his desk, and I felt a twinge of guilty pleasure thinking of the times Kenyon and I had sneaked down and ordered pizza by fax. Dad would kill us if he knew we were in his office.

The special short ring of Dad's business phone startled me for a moment and I jumped, but then I relaxed and settled down in the chair again. Dad was out and wouldn't be back until late. "Hello, you've reached the private number of Davis Design, Incorporated," Dad's voice said. "This must be important, since you've called me at home, so leave your name and number and I'll return your call as soon as it is expedient."

I couldn't help smirking. Anyone else would say, "I'll call you right back," but that wouldn't do for Dan Davis.

"Drat, Dan," a woman's voice purred over the line. "I was hoping to catch you before you left, but I suppose I haven't. I was going to have you bring the preliminary plans for the Peabody, but I'll just have to see them later." The woman paused a moment, and I could almost see her smile. "You'll be knocking at my door soon, I suppose. I'm looking forward to it." The woman laughed a delicate three-noted giggle and hung up.

Click. The red light on the answering machine began to blink, and I stared at it, my brain suddenly buzzing like a busy signal. Obviously that woman was a client or had something to do with business, but why was Dad about to knock at her door? Why did she talk in that sexy, purring voice? Why didn't she leave her name?

A crazy sort of fear gripped my heart, and I rummaged through Dad's desk drawer for half an hour until I found his address book. There was no *Peabody* listed.

Dad's battered leather briefcase stood at the side of the desk, and I fumbled with the clasps until they sprang open. Inside was the leather pocket calendar Kenyon and I had given him for Christmas last year, and on today's date, October 3, Dad had scrawled a single notation: "Benefit, 8:00 P.M., Dansk."

Dansk? Feeling like a big snoop, I flipped the address book to the "D" page. Last on the list was Alanna Dansk, 1055 Bently Park, Apt. 1015, 555-1038.

On a whim, I dialed the phone number. The phone rang four times, and as I bit my lip, I heard a breathy voice. "Hello, you've reached 555-1038. I'm sorry I'm not able to take your call just now, darling, but if you'll leave your name, I promise to ring you as soon as I'm able." The woman laughed, a delicate three-noted giggle, then sighed, "I'm looking forward to it."

My stomach did a flip-flop. Alanna Dansk was the woman who had called my father. Who was she, and why was Dad visiting her?

"What are you doing in here?"

I jumped and turned around. I had lost all track of time. Mom stood in the doorway.

I hadn't intended to tell my mother anything, but I've never been a good liar and couldn't think of an explanation for Dad's messy desk, the open briefcase, the address book, and my teacup of diet Coke. But Mom didn't even seem to notice the china; instead she calmly walked over and pressed the replay button on Dad's answering machine herself. As she listened to Alanna Dansk's message, her lips tightened into a thin line and her eyes narrowed.

"Go upstairs, Kelsey, and make sure you've finished your homework," she said, waving her arm toward the stairs. "And don't ever let me catch you using Grandma's china again."

My hands were shaking as I left Dad's office. Surely I had misunderstood something. There was a logical explanation for that phone call, and I'd hear all about it in the morning. I washed my cup and saucer, dried them, and put the china away. Then I went upstairs to brush my teeth, finish my homework, and go to bed. I knew everything would be fine in the morning.

But as I squirted toothpaste on my toothbrush, a startling

thought crossed my mind: What if there is no good explanation for that phone call? What if my dad has a *girlfriend?*

It's too terrible to think about! Worst of all, I can't tell Kenyon what I think, and there's no way Mom is going to talk about it. Even Dorian would never understand what I'm thinking now.

Is this the beginning of the end? Is it possible that my parents could get a divorce?

YOU'RE NOT ALONE

If your family has or is splitting up, you probably remember the first time you realized that things weren't OK. How did you feel when you realized your parents had problems? I asked several teenagers about what they felt:

"I remember my parents bitterly fighting with each other in their bedroom. One night Mom raced off in her car and Dad chased her. I was scared."

"I felt an emptiness inside, like something was taken away from me. I felt it was my fault the divorce happened."

"I was confused. I didn't understand why my mom had to leave."

Do any of the above voices sound familiar? Perhaps you thought problems would never happen in your family. Like Kelsey, you may have seen warning signs in your home, but you chose to ignore them. You knew things were bad, but you didn't think they were *that* bad.

Perhaps at some point you noticed that your parents had "fallen out of love" with each other. You've seen couples in love—they create a world all their own, and there are no secrets between them. But your parents weren't like those couples. They forgot to kiss each other good-bye. Your father began to spend more and more nights away from your mother. Their conversation seemed to be about superficial, unimportant, routine things. They would fight more than anything else.

Perhaps you heard complaints: "You embarrassed me tonight. Your sense of humor is all wrong." Or "I wish you would get home more nights. We never see you anymore."

Your parents, who had been each other's best friends, found other friends. Your mother began to spend all her time talking to the new friend she met at work. Your father found a new buddy down at the health club. The secrets and friendly little stories your mom and dad used to share with each other were being shared with someone else.

It became clear to your parents that something was wrong. One or both of them had a new life in another circle of friends, and the other partner may have begun the humiliating process of trying to save the marriage. He or she tried to be kinder, to do more things around the house, and to lose weight and get in shape. Your parents may have tried counseling and still couldn't find the answers.

Nothing seemed to work. The direct confrontation was painful, and the marriage was over before you knew how serious their problems were. One day the suitcases were pulled out, and the door closed behind hurried footsteps. You were left to comfort the one remaining behind.

Most people who have been through a divorce or separation will tell you that the process is grief, pure and simple. There are several stages of grief that most people pass through: denial, bargaining, anger, depression, and finally, acceptance. This book is designed to help you through those stages and through some feelings that you may not understand. It will help you realize that even though divorce is something God never wants (because he knows how much hurt it will cause), if it happens to your family, it doesn't mean he will walk away from you. Most of all, you can learn that you are not alone. There's a reason for your mixed-up feelings, and there are things you can do about them.

Your entire family could be hurt by a divorce, and it will take time for everyone to heal. Your parents may feel the same anger, guilt, hopelessness, and hurt that you feel. Even your grandparents, aunts, and uncles will feel pain. Anyone who was close to your family will be wounded and feel the grief of loss.

THERE IS HOPE

But family problems don't have to ruin *your* life. Even though you may feel like things will never be normal again and you'd rather just give up, hang in there! There are zillions of people who have been through divorce and learned to make the best of their situation. Things turned out all right for them, and they can turn out all right for you, too.

Best of all, there is someone who will tough things out with you. He loves you more than you can imagine, and he wants your life to be the best. He wants to have you as part of his family so he can strengthen you with power and his deep love. He is Jesus Christ.

You may not understand why your parents don't love each other anymore or why you feel so angry and afraid.

So if you're angry about your parents' problems . . .

If it still hurts to think about them . . .

If you're hoping they'll get back together . . .

If you feel like no one cares or understands . . .

Read on.

FOR MEMORIZATION AND MEDITATION

The Bible is more than a history book of old tales about old people. It's God's Word to us, and it can offer you comfort, instruction, and encouragement.

As we see how Kelsey handles the changes in her life and as you learn to handle the changes in your own, God's Word can remind you of important truths. At the end of each chapter in this book you'll find several verses that will work wonders in your life if you commit them to memory and spend time thinking about them. The Bible tells us to write God's Word on our heart, and while that can't be done *literally,* we can inscribe the Word of God in our mind by memorizing and meditating upon it. As you learn the verses that follow each chapter, visualize them and consider what God is saying to you through each verse.

John 16:32

Jesus felt alone, too. Jesus told his disciples about the time they would flee in fear and leave him to be crucified:

"But a time is coming, and has come, when you will be scattered, each to his own home. You will leave me all alone. Yet I am not alone, for my Father is with me."

Joshua 1:5

God promised Joshua that he would not be forsaken:

"No one will be able to stand up against you all the days of your life. As I was with Moses, so I will be with you; I will never leave you nor forsake you."

Isaiah 54:10

"'Though the mountains be shaken and the hills be removed, yet my unfailing love for you will not be shaken nor my covenant of peace be removed,' says the Lord, who has compassion on you."

The Dark Blue Volvo

I worried in silence for a week. Mom went on as usual and so did my dad, and Kenyon kept on with his pain-in-the-neck ways. I was almost jealous of him because he didn't know what I knew.

I wished the entire Alanna Dansk thing had been a bad dream, but it wasn't. Once I started looking for them, I saw little telltale signs that things weren't as they were supposed to be at home. Dad whistled more than usual around the house, and once he even brought home an armful of flowers for Mom. I was glad and thought Mom would be pleased, but she only thanked him politely and put the flowers in the sink. I was the one who finally put the wilting roses into a vase.

Mom kept to her schedule of work, PTA events, and shopping. She didn't even complain on the days when she had to pick me up from detention. *She knows I know,* I thought one day as we drove home from school. *And she's pretending that neither of us knows anything.*

Dorian knew that something was wrong with me, of course, and actually grew angry when I wouldn't tell what was bothering me. "Come on, you've been all clammed up for days now," Dorian urged as we rode home on the bus. "Is your mom mad at you about something? Did Kenyon do something?"

I glanced across the bus where Kenyon sat with his goony buddies. "No, nothing like that," I said. "I've just had something on my mind, and it's private. I'll tell you about it later, maybe."

When pigs fly, I thought to myself. *How do I tell you that I think my father has a girlfriend? You've got two parents, happy, churchgoing people, and you'd never understand what's going on in my house.*

Not that much was going on. Life *seemed* to be like usual, but I noticed for the first time that my parents didn't seem to talk much. Dad was away from home a lot, of course, and often he didn't get home until after Mom had gone to work. Sometimes he went out at night to meet with clients (or so he said) or stayed in his office working, so when Mom did come home, she didn't see him. She went up to bed, and Dad came in later. They never seemed to actually talk to each other. Even in church they sat stiffly next to each other, and their shoulders didn't even touch.

I looked out the window of the bus and sighed when we pulled up at my stop. Our house stood at the end of the street, tall and imposing. It was the biggest house on the street, the only two-story, and until last week I had been proud of it. Now it seemed lonely, with big, sad window-eyes that looked down the street as if it were envious of the other families in the other houses.

Kenyon bounded off the bus; I stepped down the steps slowly and forced myself to turn and wave good-bye to Dorian. "Hey, whose car is that at our house?" Kenyon called, turning around to yell at me. "Were we expecting company?"

I squinted at the boxy, dark blue car in the driveway, a

Volvo. "I don't think so," I answered, shrugging. "It'll be someone for Mom or Dad, though, and it won't have anything to do with us."

I was 100 percent wrong. The stranger in the blue car changed our lives completely.

He was a big man in a faded blue suit that seemed too hot for a Florida afternoon. He stirred uncomfortably when Kenyon and I came in through the front door, but Mom didn't budge from the couch. "It's OK, Mr. Kincaid, the children are going to know about this sooner or later," she said, her voice oddly flat. "Come on in, kids, and have a seat."

I felt almost sorry for Kenyon; he looked honestly bewildered. We sat next to each other on the couch across from Mom, while Mr. Kincaid fidgeted in a wing chair. I noticed that Mom held a manila envelope in her hands, and the edges of photographs peeked out from the open end. "Mr. Kincaid is a private detective that I hired last week," Mom explained simply. "Your father is having an affair with one of his clients. I am asking him to leave the house tonight, and I want a divorce. I'm sorry it has to be this way, kids, but I don't know a gentle way to say this."

Mr. Kincaid stirred uncomfortably and cleared his throat. "If that's all you need, Mrs. Davis, I'll go now," he said, standing. "Do you want me to send you a statement?"

"I'll pay you now," Mom said, setting the envelope on the coffee table. "Come with me into the kitchen, and I'll get my checkbook."

They left the room, and Kenyon sank back into the couch cushions, his mouth opened in amazement. I reached for the envelope and shook out the photographs. They were black-and-white prints of my father with an attractive blonde woman. In one shot they were sitting at a table together, in another they were entering an apartment building. I flipped through the pictures until I found one of Dad kissing the woman in his car—then my stomach churned, and I threw the pictures on the floor.

"That's disgusting," I said, clenching my teeth as my cheeks burned with shame. "It's embarrassing! How could Dad do something like this?"

"I don't believe it," Kenyon murmured. "The old man let himself get caught! How could sharp ol' Dan Davis be so stupid?"

"Take a look at those," I said, my finger shaking as I pointed to the photographs. "I knew that something was going on a week ago. That woman called and left a message on Dad's business machine."

"Why didn't you say anything?" Kenyon asked, and for the first time I really looked at my brother. Something had come up behind his eyes, a kind of wall, and I thought he didn't want to believe, he wasn't ready to believe the truth.

"I didn't want to tell you," I whispered, "because I didn't want it to be true. I guess it is."

~~~~~~~~~~~~~~

Kenyon and I were upstairs when Dad came home, and when he abruptly stopped whistling, we knew he had run into Mom. Without wanting to, we crept out of our rooms to the staircase, where we sat like twin statues and listened to our parents rage at each other from the living room.

"I know everything about Alanna Dansk," Mother said flatly, "and I want you out of here tonight. I want a divorce as soon as possible. And I'm keeping the house and my car and the kids. You forfeited it all, Dan, when you gave that woman a second glance."

Dad gasped and drew in his breath, and I could close my eyes and imagine his reaction. He would be shocked, then he would try to cover things up with his casual coolness. But what Dad actually said surprised me.

"All right, Barbara, have it your way. I could lie, you know, because it all began perfectly innocently. Alanna was working with me on the Peabody Hotel project—she likes my work and wanted me to get the bid to design the building. Things just got out of hand, I guess, and—"

"*How-could-you-do-this-to-us?*" Mom's voice was like a machine gun, her words spraying furiously. Her calm had vanished in an instant, and I bit my lip when she broke and began to sob.

"I'm sorry for the kids," Dad answered. "But I just don't care about our marriage anymore, Barbara. Alanna makes me feel alive, and I really need that feeling right now. What we had—you and I—has been gone for years. You have your work and your PTA; I have my work, and now Alanna's a part of my life. But I never meant to hurt you."

"You can stop lying now," Mom answered, her voice strangled. "You meant to hurt us all. You knew what you were doing, and you did it anyway."

There was a long pause, then I heard Dad say softly, "I'll get the things I need for tonight and come back for the rest of my things on the weekend. Leave a message at the office if you need me."

Then he was at the bottom of the stairs looking up at us, and Kenyon and I stiffened. What were we supposed to say? Dad came up the stairs slowly, placing his hands on our heads as he walked woodenly by. "I don't expect you to understand," he said, without looking down at us, "but I'll always love you two."

Ten minutes later he was gone, and I went to my room and

cried. I've seen a part of my parents' lives that is so shocking, so dirty, and so ugly—I never want to come out of my room again. I'm too ashamed.

DIVORCE FEELS LIKE A DIRTY WORD

Denial, shame, embarrassment—divorce brings all three to your life.

When one of your parents first walked out, you probably hoped the situation would only be temporary, but things went from bad to worse. Well-meaning friends stopped by the house and told your upset parent, "Forget it. You're better off alone than with someone who doesn't appreciate you."

You thought maybe your wandering parent would find the world a difficult place and come to his or her senses and return home. But it didn't happen. The friends, the job—everything he or she needed was out there, already in place.

Meanwhile you went to school and tried to concentrate on schoolwork. You told your friends your mom or dad was away on business or visiting a relative; you told your best friend the truth. Your best friend nodded sympathetically and patted you on the shoulder; five minutes later he or she was trying to cheer you up and "take your mind off it." As if you could forget about it!

You worried. You found yourself wondering where the family would spend Thanksgiving this year, how you would divide your Christmases, and if you'd be getting an eighteen-year-old step-mother. Would you ever eat dinner together again as a family?

"More than anything I was ashamed," Vera says. "Ashamed of living in that crummy place and ashamed of my parents for splitting up. I didn't tell a soul. One day in class I broke down. The teacher kept me after class, and I told him why I was feeling so upset. He was a Christian. If he hadn't been there, I don't know what I might have done."[1]

18

It doesn't matter how old you are when your parents decide to get a divorce, you still feel ashamed. Linda Francke was an adult when her parents divorced, and she knows divorce is humiliating at any age. "It's embarrassing to see your sixty-year-old father running around with a woman young enough to be your sister," she says.[2]

Some kids not only have to face their friends and relatives but an entire church as well. What if your parents were Christians and leaders in the church? Christians are supposed to be strong enough to resist temptation, so why do so many of them commit adultery and ruin their marriages? Even those famous TV preachers have problems! But Christians are people, and people often fail. Many Christians fail to honor their marriages, and they divorce.

After a divorce, many kids feel alienated from members of the church and God himself. They have trouble understanding how God could allow the divorce to happen, and one of their biggest problems is carrying the load of guilt—aren't Christians supposed to have happy marriages? Aren't Christians supposed to be able to hand their troubles over to God and not worry about them? You may dread going to church if you think you can't live up to the "happy Christian" ideal.

But there's wisdom in the old saying that the church isn't a haven for saints, it's a hospital for sinners. Divorce is far from God's ideal, but it happens a lot today. People are people—and people fail. It is very likely that you haven't faced anything that hasn't happened to someone in your church. And just maybe that someone else can help you heal the hurts in your heart because he or she knows what you're thinking and feeling.

WHAT HAPPENED TO YOUR HAPPY HOME?

Because your parents have split up, you may think back to happy Christmases and birthdays and wonder if those happy times were based upon a lie. You may question the love on which your family was built. Did your parents ever really love each other? When your dad sent flowers to your mom, did he do it because he loved her or because he was trying to cover up like Kelsey's dad?

Chances are the happier your home life was before the divorce, the harder it will be for you to handle the breakup of your parents. If your parents did nothing but fight, maybe the quiet will be welcome, although it may be disturbingly strange. If one of your parents was an alcoholic or abusive, perhaps a little peace will do you good. But it may not feel "right" at first.

One young man told me about his parents' breakup: "I was nine, and I did not really know what 'divorce' meant. However, I remember my parents bitterly fighting with each other in their bedroom. One night Mom raced off in her car and Dad chased her. I was scared. It got so bad another time that the police came. I was relieved to see a calm policeman trying to help."

Cody's parents divorced when he was two; he never met his father as a child. Even though he is now grown, he still remembers what it felt like to be a child of divorce: "I remember having feelings that I was different because I didn't have a dad. Most of the other kids whose parents were divorced at least knew where their dads were, but I had no idea about mine.

"Today, though, it's extremely undignified to come to school and have people find out that your parents are divorcing. Most kids don't want to tell anybody. When I grew up as a divorced kid, I still had my family—aunts, uncles, and cousins. People would walk down the street, see me, and say, 'Aren't you Cody? I know your grandmother.' People just don't do that anymore."

DO YOU FEEL ALL ALONE?

Do you feel isolated? You're probably bussed to school, your parent works, your cousins live all over the country, and you may not know your neighbors. So who can you talk to about your family?

Maybe you don't want to talk. You may think that no one can understand what you are feeling. You probably have friends who are in a similar situation, but they don't know about *your* family. You feel all alone, and it really hurts, doesn't it?

You need to find a good way to cope with all that you're feeling. The bad feelings won't go away by themselves, and time may not heal the wounds you received when your family broke up. There are lots of ways to cope, and some ways are better than others. Take this little "coping" test and decide which of the following best describes you:

___ "The divorce has made me miserable, so I'll just crawl into a shell and not say much to anyone. I'll withdraw."

___ "The divorce has made me so angry that sometimes I feel like I'm mad at the world! Since no one really cares about me, I'll just look out for myself and fight anyone who gets in my way."

___ "I'm not going to let anyone know how much I'm hurting inside. If I'm happy and clown around a lot, I can fool them all. Maybe I can even fool myself into thinking that everything's OK."

___ "This divorce isn't really happening. My dad is just going away on business or something, and my folks will work out their problems one of these days. Until then, I'll deny reality and trust that things will work out."

___ "This divorce is just too different. I'll pretend that my family is just like everyone else's. I'll conform to my friends so they won't know how different I feel inside."

___ "This divorce hurt me so much, but I'll compensate for the pain by being the best at everything else. I'll get good grades and help my mom, I'll be the best at everything at school, and everyone will think I've really got my act together.

Which of the above methods of coping have you chosen? Have you withdrawn from life? Do you walk around with an angry "chip" on your shoulder? Have you become the class clown? Are you denying reality and lying to yourself and your friends? Or maybe you're just conforming to the crowd or directing all your energies into becoming an overachiever?

How are your parents coping with the divorce? Does your mom deny reality, constantly talking about the day your father will come back? Has your dad become withdrawn, skipping work and staying away from his friends? Which coping methods have they chosen?

Perhaps you're frightened by the changes you see in your parents. Maybe they're hostile one moment and depressed the next. They may be so consumed by their emotions that they don't notice what you're going through. Often parents think, *Oh, the kids are tough. They'll get over it. After all, they still have two parents. It's not like somebody died.*

But it is. A marriage died, and a family feels the pain.

After a divorce it is very likely that the parent you live with will be concerned first and foremost with survival. *How am I going to pay the bills?* your mother may wonder. *Will I be frightened to live without a man in the house? How am I going to face the future?*

Divorce will bring fear, embarrassment, and insecurity not only to you, but to your parents as well.

FOR MEMORIZATION AND MEDITATION

Jeremiah 29:11-13

"'For I know the plans I have for you,'" declares the Lord, "'plans to prosper you and not to harm you, plans to give you hope and a future. Then you will call upon me and come and pray to me, and I will listen to you. You will seek me and find me when you seek me with all your heart.'"

My Love Letter

I glared at the woman in the photograph. "I hate you, Alanna Dansk!" I muttered, jabbing my fingernail into the woman's smiling face. "It's all your fault!"

From where he lay on the couch, Kenyon snorted. "How can you blame her?" he said. "It's Dad who was so hot to cheat on Mom."

"Sometimes I think it's our fault somehow," I answered. "I mean, if Dad didn't have to work so hard to get the money to raise two teenagers, maybe he would never have met this woman. You know how he's always complaining about bills. My braces, your football equipment—"

"You can blame yourself if you want, but I still think Dad's a crud," Kenyon answered. "Mom would be right if she never took him back."

"How can you say that?" I whirled around from the desk where I had been trying to do my homework. (That was a wasted effort; I haven't been able to concentrate on school at all since my dad left. I have racked up two weeks' worth of F's, and I'll have an absolutely *outstanding* report card next month. Mom will probably ground me for the rest of the year.)

I let my unfinished algebra paper flutter to the floor. "Dad just has to come back. Things aren't right here without him.

Mom can't sleep at night; I hear her up walking around at three o'clock in the morning. I haven't passed a single test since Dad left, and you haven't done anything but lie on the couch and watch TV."

Kenyon aimed the remote control at the television and flicked through several channels. "So? It's my life."

"So you're just going to become a zombie? Ken, we've got to do something to get Mom and Dad back together. This Alanna bimbo is nothing compared to Mom. If we just concentrate on trying to get Dad to come back home, he'll come. He'll forget all about that woman, and things will be back the way they're supposed to be."

Kenyon didn't answer at first, and I thought maybe he hadn't been listening. But after a minute he raised his head from the couch and looked at me. "So what do we do?"

"I dunno," I answered. "Maybe first we could just tell him we miss him. Then he'll feel so guilty about leaving us he'll come back, and he and Mom will have plenty of time to work things out."

"I'll help, Kels, but I can't do that," Kenyon answered, sitting up. His blue eyes were earnest. "I can't lie and tell him I miss him because right now I'm so mad at him I could jack his jaw with pleasure. But you can do it, and I promise I won't slug him if he shows up here."

"How do I do it?" I asked aloud.

"Call him," Kenyon suggested.

I bit my lip. "No. That woman might answer. Or I might get upset and start crying."

"Well, you can't go see him. You'd start crying for sure."

"I'll write him a letter," I answered. By instinct I headed to Dad's office for a piece of paper, but the empty room mocked me when I reached it. His desk, his chair, his drafting table were all gone.

I walked slowly back to my stack of schoolbooks and ripped a fresh sheet of paper from my notebook. Here's what I wrote:

Dear Dad:

I know things were bad the other night when you left, but Kenyon and I want you to know we miss you very, very much. Mom has been upset, too, and we think she was just letting off steam when she said she wanted a divorce. Kenyon and I don't want a divorce. We want you to come home.

School has been awful and Mom can't sleep and Kenyon just lies around on the couch and watches reruns, so come home, Dad, and come soon.

Love,
Kelsey

WHOSE FAULT IS IT?

How did you hear about your parents' breakup? Maybe they called you in and said, "You'd better sit down. We want to talk to you." After a pause and a deep breath, one or both of your parents said, "We're getting a divorce." If your parents didn't tell you directly, you probably found out when your dad moved into an apartment or your mom simply said she wasn't coming home again.

Even though you may have known a breakup was coming and you could see the signs of a family falling apart, hearing someone actually say the word *divorce* probably made you feel a little sick to your stomach. Your next reaction may have been resistance: *This can't be happening. Whatever caused it, I'll find a way to make it better. There has to be something I can do.*

COULD IT HAVE BEEN YOUR FAULT?

Do you feel like you did something to cause your parents' breakup? Like Kelsey and Kenyon, most kids think they had at least *something* to do with it.

You may not have known *what* you did, but maybe for a while you tried to be perfect so your parents wouldn't be upset. After a while you realized even your angelic behavior meant nothing to your parents' marriage. They may have been too wrapped up in their angry and hurt feelings toward each other to even notice your efforts.

Most younger kids naturally assume they are to blame for the divorce. "Almost three-quarters of the six-year-olds we studied blame themselves for the divorce," child psychologist Neil Kalter told *USA Today.* "That is one reason they are so quiet. They feel awful about having done such a bad thing and they don't want anyone to discover what they have done."[1]

If you have younger brothers or sisters, they might think the divorce happened because of one single event—one night, one fight, or one wrong move. After the breakup they may even begin to think that just one wrong action on their part will destroy their remaining family relationships. They could be afraid that one goof will ruin their lives all over again.

Teenagers often blame themselves for divorce because as a marriage deteriorates, people in the family tend to fight more among themselves. There is pressure in the air—kids fight with their brothers and sisters and with their parents. When things are at their roughest, everyone snaps at everyone else for no reason at all.

You need to know (underline this!) that *you are not to blame for your parents' divorce.* If your parents should happen to tell you something like, "If you hadn't been so hard to handle, we wouldn't have split up," *disagree!* Your parents are adults. As parents and as adults they should know how to handle their problems. They are trying to dump a load of guilt on you that should not be yours! It may make your confused and hurt parents feel better to blame you, but *parents do not divorce because of their children.* They divorce because they decide to do so.

Kathy Callahan-Howell wrote that a family member once approached her and said, "If you would just go to your father and put your arms around him, and ask him to come back, he would."[2] Has someone put that kind of pressure on you? Suddenly it isn't your parents' responsibility to either part as friends or mend their marriage; the entire burden is placed on your shoulders! Don't let anyone do that to you. You are the child, not the parent.

While you're sorting out your feelings about the divorce, try to realize that the divorce didn't happen because of one single event. There may have been one night when your parents had a big blowup and one walked out, but most likely their problems had been simmering for a long, long time. That one argument you heard was simply the logical explosion of many problems that had not been solved.

There were probably family fights and difficult days when you and your parents did things you regret. Ask forgiveness for those wrongs, and don't dwell on them anymore. Jesus Christ offers complete forgiveness for all sins, and if you are a Christian, you can call on his perfect forgiveness anytime. Jesus Christ will never leave you, never blame you, and never forsake you if you are a child of his.

IF I'M NOT TO BLAME, WHO IS?

I asked a large group of teenagers who they blamed for their parents' divorce. Among the responses were "alcohol," "my father," "my mother," "my dad's girlfriend," and "everything."

If your parents were fighting before the breakup, they probably blame each other for their troubles. If you didn't blame yourself, you probably want to blame the parent who initiated the separation or the one who walked out first.

But you need to understand that in most cases both parents contribute to the difficulties of their marriage. If your father was having an affair with another woman, perhaps the love between him and your mother had been allowed to die years before. I certainly don't want to excuse anyone for having an extramarital affair. Adultery is definitely wrong and one of the quickest ways to destroy a family. But love in marriage doesn't have to die and shouldn't be allowed to. So while one person may take things farther than the other, both the husband and the wife usually contribute to whatever problems there are.

Divorce occurs when two adults are unable to solve their problems. That's the bottom line. It's not necessary for you to understand all the messy details, but you should know what problems there were and why they couldn't be worked out.

It may be that the parent who walked out of your home had put up with years of abuse, neglect, or humiliation. You only know a few aspects of your parents' personalities as married people. You can only guess at what they were like before you were born, and you do not know what they do and say when they are alone together and totally honest with one another. They may have been putting on a mask "for the sake of the children," and you may not know your parents very well at all.

It isn't easy to get away from this issue of blame. Perhaps one parent didn't agree to a divorce; maybe one forced a divorce on the other. That situation can make it easy to blame one parent; but remember, it usually takes two to destroy a marriage, and it's human nature to blame someone else when we fail. That's what makes divorce so angry, bitter, and destructive.

FOR MEMORIZATION AND MEDITATION

Philippians 2:14-15

"Do everything without complaining or arguing, so that you may become blameless and pure, children of God without fault in a crooked and depraved generation, in which you shine like stars in the universe."

1 Corinthians 4:5

"Therefore judge nothing before the appointed time; wait till the Lord comes. He will bring to light what is hidden in darkness and will expose the motives of men's hearts. At that time each will receive his praise from God."

CHAPTER F O U R
The Neon Rose

K elsey and Kenyon Davis, please report to the school office." The secretary's voice on the intercom interrupted my reading and I glanced quickly at Kenyon, who had been talking to his best friend, Chad. Kenyon caught my eye, raised an eyebrow, and shrugged.

Mrs. Whiteside looked up from her paperwork. "I guess you two should go to the office," she said, smiling. "Too bad you didn't get called up sooner. The bell rings in just two minutes."

I waited for Kenyon to join me out in the hall. "Why are we going to the office now?" I asked, my throat tightening. "Do you think something's happened to Mom? I remember in sixth grade they came and got Dave Bradley out of class, and his mother had just been in a bad car wreck."

"It's nothing like that," Kenyon answered casually, but I noticed that he began to walk faster. I lengthened my steps to keep up with him. What was going on?

The dismissal bell rang before we reached the office, and I felt like I was swimming upstream as I followed Kenyon through the swarm of kids who were headed out to the parking lot. Finally, though, we made it to the office, and my eyes widened when I saw our dad waiting for us in the waiting area.

33

"Hi, guys," Dad said, standing up. "I wanted to take you two out after school, and I had to get you before you got on the bus."

"Is Mom OK?" Kenyon asked, his voice cracking. "Nothing is wrong, is it?"

Dad smiled a lopsided smile. "No, everything's fine. I checked with her, and she knows I'm bringing you home later. What do you say? Shall we go for burgers at the Neon Rose Café?"

Ordinarily I would have flipped; the Neon Rose was absolutely my favorite restaurant in the world. Their napkins were pale pink and folded to look like rosebuds, and they gave roses to all the ladies who ate there. But eating at the Neon Rose without Mom wouldn't be the same.

"Whatever you say," Kenyon replied, his voice cool.

When we were seated in a booth, Dad cleared his throat and folded his hands in front of him. "I got your letter yesterday," he said, nodding in my direction, "and I thought it was time I had a talk with my two favorite kids."

I couldn't look away from Dad, but I could feel Kenyon stiffen beside me.

"Kids, I'm your father, and I always will be. I loved you the day you were born, and I will always love you. The relationship between us will never change, no matter what happens between me and your mother."

I looked down at my napkin. Kenyon began to jiggle his legs nervously.

"I can't come home. I appreciate your wanting me to come home, but I've taken an apartment downtown, and you can come stay with me there on weekends if you like." Dad

34

leaned forward and patted my hand. "You can help me decorate the place, Kels. It needs a woman's touch."

"What about that other woman?" Kenyon's voice was bitter. "Is she living there, too?"

Dad leaned back and shook his head. "No, Son, she's not. I thought I needed some time alone."

"Why didn't you think of that earlier?" Kenyon spat out the words. "Why'd you ever look at this woman? Mom has worked for you, cleaned your clothes, cooked your food, made your bed, vacuumed your house, and you're trading her in for a younger model!"

"Is that how you see it?" I could hear anger rising in my dad's voice. "Is that what your mother told you? If it is, it's not a true picture, Son. You have to remember there are two sides to every story. You have to see things from both—"

"Don't tell me what I see! I *know* what I see!" Kenyon was almost yelling, and I winced. It was a good thing it was early; there weren't many people in the restaurant.

Dad didn't even look around. He kept his eyes firmly locked on Kenyon's. "What do you see, Son?"

Kenyon's face flushed, and his eyes filled with angry tears. "I see a selfish man who never really loved his family. You were never at home when we needed you, 'cause you were always off somewhere building something. Mom works around the house for you all day, then works at the store all night—"

"Your mother *wants* to work," Dad inserted. "She doesn't have to work."

"Yes, she does!" Kenyon went on. "It gives her something to do at night 'cause you're never home! You've always got to have the best of everything—the best house, the best golf clubs, the best office, the prettiest secretary, and now you've decided Mom's not the best! Well, you're wrong, and I hate you for what you've done!"

"Your mother asked *me* to leave," Dad answered calmly, tapping the table with his manicured fingernails.

"It was *you* who had affairs!" Kenyon shot back. "And I know about the others, too! I never said anything, but I've heard you talking on the phone with other women!"

I stared at my brother as my brain hummed. Other women? How long had this been going on?

Dad's face flushed red. "What are you talking about?"

Kenyon's voice trembled: "I used to want to be just like you, Dad. You wouldn't let us in your office at home, but I'd crawl in when you weren't looking and lie on the carpet in front of your desk, just so I could hear you talk on the phone to your clients. I thought you were great, until the day I heard you arrange a date with some other woman."

I couldn't believe what Kenyon was saying, but he kept on mercilessly. "I knew it wasn't Mom on the phone because she was upstairs. After that, I sneaked down there lots of times to see what you were doing because I wanted to warn Mom if I could. But I never did."

"Our marriage died a long time ago," Dad said, spreading his hands. "I don't think you can understand."

"No, I don't think I can," Kenyon answered. The waitress appeared at the table with menus in her hand, but Kenyon slid out of the booth and stood up. "Excuse me, but I've lost my appetite. If you want to stay here and eat, Kels, that's fine. I'm going to walk home."

Kenyon turned and stalked out of the restaurant with long strides, and my father glanced apologetically at the waitress. "I'm terribly sorry," he said, placing a five-dollar bill on the table. "But it looks like we won't be eating today. We'll be back another time." He glanced at me. "Are you coming, Kels?"

I left my rosebud napkin on the table.

TOO ANGRY FOR WORDS

Divorce brings out anger like nothing else. Your mother, your father, your brothers and sisters, even you may be too angry for words. Most teenagers I interviewed said they were "hurt, confused, and angry" when they first realized their parents were breaking up.

Why does divorce make people angry? Sometimes people develop anger as a defense mechanism to cover the hurt they feel. They think they've been rejected, and their pride has been deeply wounded. Men, women, and children lash out in anger when they are deeply hurt like an injured animal made vicious by pain.

Admit it—doesn't anger feel good sometimes? When we work ourselves up into a good temper tantrum, we feel justified. How dare someone hurt us! We may later regret the things we do or say in anger, but while we're mad, it feels good to unload our feelings onto someone else.

Anger brings a sudden flush of adrenaline, excitement, and a feeling of nervous power. It affects your emotions, your body, and your spirit. Anger can be a monster, ready to devour whoever hurt you, but if you keep it alive too long, it can gobble you up as well.

WHAT'S YOUR ANGER LIKE?

When you get angry, do you have a roaring "mad spell" or are you more of a "slow burner"? Is the anger you feel about your parents' divorce intense, or is it more undefined and undirected?

Many young people don't know exactly what they are feeling during a divorce, and anger seems to be the only recognizable emotion. But your anger may be masking confusion, fear, disappointment, sadness, or loneliness.

My husband, Gary, is a youth pastor, and he once worked with Trent, an outgoing, athletic kid. Trent enjoyed coming to our church, and we loved him. One Sunday he came to church in a black mood. He was quiet and sullen. Before too long Trent was involved in an argument with one of our adult workers. Gary was perplexed—what had happened to Trent? What could possibly cause this kind of change in such a great kid?

After church Gary caught Trent alone. "What's wrong with you today?" he asked.

Trent's angry face quivered, and his hard expression broke. He began to cry and whispered, "My dad left last night. He's not coming back."

ANGER COVERS ALL

With which of the following statements would you agree?

____ I wish my dad was home again.

____ I wish my mom and dad would get together again.

____ It makes me feel angry to see them fighting.

____ I am angry because my family will never be the same.

Were you angry when your parents divorced? What were the things that made you angry? Take a moment to get a pen and paper and list everything that happened during the divorce that made you angry.

I know your anger did not begin the day your parents separated nor did it end the day of the final divorce decree. You may still be angry. What are the things making you angry now? Are you angry because

- your father or mother is dating;
- money is tighter than it used to be;
- your parents fight about you;
- Mom or Dad seems to resent you;
- you have a new home or a new school;
- your new stepmother or stepfather has different rules;
- your friends don't seem to understand what you're feeling;
- you feel different from other kids with "normal" families;
- your grades have fallen and your parents are complaining;
- you are now living with stepbrothers or stepsisters?

Did any of the above things ring a bell? Make an honest list of the things that are bothering you. Now put your list aside for a few moments.

POINT OF VIEW: THE GREAT EYE-OPENER

Have you ever tried seeing a situation from another person's point of view? There's an old Indian prayer you may have heard: "Great Spirit, help me not to criticize another man until I have walked a mile in his moccasins." In other words, perhaps we wouldn't be so angry with people or situations if we could see things from a different perspective.

It isn't easy to give up your point of view even for a minute, especially if you are convinced that you're right. But give it a try. It takes real maturity. Small children believe the world revolves around their needs and desires, but you are older and know there is another viewpoint to all situations. In fact, wisdom is some-times defined as "seeing things from God's perspective." If you are willing, you can learn to see things as God sees them.

Take a moment to think about this chapter from Mr. Davis's perspective. What was he thinking and feeling when he took Kelsey and Kenyon out to the Neon Rose? Did he have good intentions when he picked them up at school? Does he still love the twins? Why did he think it was important to spend some time alone with them? Why does he feel he can't go home? Obviously Mr. Davis knows that Kenyon is upset and angry, but could Mr. Davis be angry, too? Does he have a right to be angry at Kenyon? Why or why not?

THINK ABOUT OTHERS

Have you stopped to consider the feelings of everyone in your situation? How do you think your mother feels now? Is she angry with you? Why or why not? Is she angry with your father? Why?

How does your father feel? Is he angry, and with whom is he angry? Ask him what he is feeling.

How about the man your mother is dating or the woman your father is dating? How does your stepfather feel when you say hateful things to him? Does he know how you feel when he tries to discipline you? Do you know how he feels when you rebel and refuse to accept his leadership? What does he bring to your mother's life? Don't just guess—ask her!

If you do not know what is going on in the minds of the adults in your life, you may feel detached, neglected, or totally marooned in your own family. Once you may have been the center of attention, but now your parents' energy is visibly directed toward someone else. But instead of building up anger about the situation, talk to your parents. They haven't stopped loving you.

ANGER AND HOSTILITY

Susan Grobman, a child of divorce, wrote about her feelings of anger and hostility:

> Sometimes I am obnoxious to [my father], for I believe he was dishonest with my family for many years. I could accept the fact that he found someone whom he loved more than my mother. However, I never can forget that he deceived three people who loved and trusted him. Instead of telling my mother when he initially developed the relationship outside our home, he decided to go behind our backs until we found out ourselves. I sometimes think that everyone in the neighborhood knew before us.[1]

Do you ever want to be hateful to your mom or dad? Are you upset by these feelings? Don't be. God gave us emotions. It is OK to feel angry, and it is OK to cry (even for guys!). God loves you just as you are, and your parents do too.

But sometimes in divorce we think we have to hide all our feelings. It's like the time one of my boyfriends ran over my dog and killed her. I really loved that puppy, but she lay there in the road, dead. I wanted to cry because my puppy was dead, but I didn't want to make my boyfriend feel bad. So I said something like, "That's OK. It was an accident," when I wanted to scream, "You dummy! Didn't you look under the car? You just killed my dog, and I loved her!"

DEALING WITH YOUR ANGER

There are lots of things in life that just aren't fair. You're going to be angry lots of times for lots of different reasons. What's the best way to deal with anger?

41

First, make sure your anger is directed at a problem, not at people. Be angry at the divorce, not at the people involved. Anger directed toward people becomes hostility and hate. No one is happy with a heart full of hate.

Though it is natural to be angry sometimes, don't let anger fill your mind for too long. Anger can easily grow into bitterness, and bitterness will poison your outlook in every aspect of life.

The Bible tells us, "In your anger do not sin" (Psalm 4:4; Ephesians 4:26). You can judge whether your anger is leading you to sin or not by examining two areas: What *makes you angry* and what *anger makes you.*

If you are angry when you see sin or a problem that's ruining someone's life, that is not necessarily bad anger. Jesus himself was very angry when he threw the money changers out of the temple because they had distorted the meaning of worship. He was righteously angry, turning over tables and scowling at those who used God's temple for their own selfish purposes.

But if you are angry because someone has hurt your pride or deprived you of some selfish desire, you must learn how to be angry and not react in the wrong way. For instance, if you blow up at your mom because she said you couldn't go out on a school night, you are angry because *your* desires weren't granted. Your angry response is the direct opposite of what God would have you do because you are to honor and obey your parents. If you've blown up in a similar situation, you need to apologize and set the matter straight.

What can anger do? It can make you bitter, jealous, resentful, hardhearted, joyless, grumpy, and a real pain to be around. Would you like to be known as the Scrooge of your class? Anger is even hard on your body! Anger can cause or aggravate ulcers, high blood pressure, headaches, and other illnesses.

"Anger resides in the lap of fools," says Ecclesiastes 7:9. In 1 John 4:20-21 we read, "If anyone says, 'I love God,' yet hates his brother [or parent, or stepparent], he is a liar. For anyone who does not love his brother [or parent, or stepparent], whom he has seen, cannot love God, whom he has not seen. And he has given us this command: Whoever loves God must also love his brother [or parent, or stepparent]."

The Bible tells us there is a time for everything:

> *A time to be born and a time to die,*
> *a time to plant and a time to uproot,*
> *a time to kill and a time to heal,*
> *a time to tear down and a time to build,*
> *a time to weep and a time to laugh,*
> *a time to mourn and a time to dance,*
> *a time to scatter stones and a time to gather them,*
> *a time to embrace and a time to refrain,*
> *a time to search and a time to give up,*
> *a time to keep and a time to throw away,*
> *a time to tear and a time to mend,*
> *a time to be silent and a time to speak,*
> *a time to love and a time to hate,*
> *a time for war and a time for peace.*
> *—Ecclesiastes 3:2-8*

After a divorce there is a time to grieve and a time to cry. But soon it will be time to heal. Let go of any anger you feel toward your parents. Remember, they hurt, too. They've been angry, just like you. It's time to move on.

FOR MEMORIZATION AND MEDITATION

Psalm 4:4

"In your anger do not sin; when you are on your beds, search your hearts and be silent."

Ecclesiastes 7:9

"Do not be quickly provoked in your spirit, for anger resides in the lap of fools."

Ephesians 4:26

"'In your anger do not sin': Do not let the sun go down while you are still angry."

1 John 4:20-21

"If anyone says, 'I love God,' yet hates his brother, he is a liar. For anyone who does not love his brother, whom he has seen, cannot love God, whom he has not seen. And he has given us this command: Whoever loves God must also love his brother."

House for Sale

I was awakened on Monday morning by a rhythmic thumping coming from the front lawn. "What in the world?" I muttered, staggering out of bed. I reached the window and pulled back the curtain. On the grass in front of the house, a man in a gold jacket was hammering a huge For Sale sign into our lawn.

That woke me up. "Mom!" I yelled, not moving from the window. "Come quick! Some guy's trying to sell our house!"

Kenyon emerged from his room, his eyes still puffy from sleep. "What are you yelling about?" he demanded, scratching his chest. "It's seven o'clock, for heaven's sake."

"Look out the window," I said, pulling the curtain open wider. "Some guy's obviously got the wrong house. He's hammered a sale sign into our front lawn."

Mom came into the room then, all dressed up in a suit. Her hair was combed and curled to perfection, and I nearly fell over. My mother never dresses up like that, not even to go to work at the store.

"Goodness, but that man is early," Mom said, adjusting the sleeve on her cuff. "But the earlier, the better, I guess. With any luck, the house will sell by Christmas, and we won't have to move during the holidays. Say your prayers, kids, and maybe everything will work out on schedule."

"Moo-ve?" Kenyon croaked out the word. He sounded like a sleepy cow.

I shook my head. "What do you mean, *move? We* can't be moving."

"Yes, I'm afraid we have to." Mom sank onto my unmade bed. "You see, according to the divorce settlement, the equity in the house is to be split between your father and me. He'll pay child support until you two are eighteen, and he's promised to help with your college expenses. But I'm going to get a full-time job and support myself. I don't want to live off your father one day longer than I have to."

"The divorce settlement?" I felt my knees grow weak. "You really are getting a divorce?"

Mom stared steadily at me. Her eyes didn't waver once. "Of course, dear, where have you been? I have my lawyer and your father has his, and things should be settled in about a month. In the meantime, though, we have to sell the house, so I expect you two to help me keep this place cleaned up and neat. We'll have people coming through here at all hours."

She stood up and jerked her thumb toward Kenyon's room. "Under the bed, young man, are several subspecies of plant and animal growth, so I'd like to see that room clean by the time I get back from my appointments today. With any luck, I'll have a new job by the end of the week, so we'll celebrate this weekend, OK?"

Mom turned and walked downstairs. Kenyon and I stared after her. "Things aren't working out the way I thought they would," I whispered. "I really thought Dad would come home."

"Guess you were wrong," Kenyon answered, absently scratching his chest again. "I guess we were all wrong. There are going to be a lot of changes around here."

He shuffled lazily into the bathroom, and I sat on my bed

and hugged my favorite stuffed animal, Gooch. What was it my mother had said? "Say your prayers, kids"? Could God really help in a situation like this? If God wanted to help, why hadn't he brought my dad home? Why had he even allowed this whole mess to happen?

Even though I didn't understand, I hugged Gooch and closed my eyes. "God, if you can help, we would appreciate it," I whispered. "I don't want my parents to divorce. I don't want to move. I can't handle all these changes." I paused. Was that too selfish a prayer? I had to admit, I hadn't been exactly on the best of terms with God. I hadn't read my Bible in weeks, and sometimes I only prayed when I really wanted something. Maybe this is all my fault and God is just trying to get my attention.

I closed my eyes again. "I'm sorry, God, for not being as close to you as I should be. We're in a mess, Lord, and we're your children, so please don't leave us now."

I put Gooch down on the bed and went back to the window. God hadn't whisked the real-estate man away; he was still there, squinting up at the house and making notes in a little book. I knew that unless God intervened with a miracle, we'd be in a new house soon. If we moved to a new house, Kenyon and I might have to go to a new school. If we went to a new school, I'd have to make all new friends.

Life isn't fair. I didn't ask for all these changes, but the divorce is bringing them my way.

DIVORCE CHANGES THINGS

Divorce brings a lot of things, but more than anything it brings change. Change can be confusing, frightening, depressing, and bewildering.

Joshua told me about the time when he was eight years old and his parents called a pastor to come over and talk to the family's three children. While Josh's parents walked around the block, the pastor tried to explain to the kids that his parents were going to separate for a while, perhaps forever.

Josh knew his dad had been drinking and spending a lot of money on alcohol, and he had seen his mother emerge from their bedroom with eyes red from crying. But he was confused. Why did his dad have to leave? Things had been as they were for years and years, so why were his parents breaking up now? The idea of change scared Josh a lot.

The changes that come from divorce can be frightening. "To change," says *Webster's Dictionary,* is "to make radically different; to give a different position, course, direction to; or to replace with another." We change our clothes, change a tire, and change classes at school, but those are minor changes. Divorce brings major, big-time changes.

You may not want your family to become radically different or replace one parent with another. You may rebel at the thought of going to a different school or living in a different place or knowing that a different man is sleeping with your mom. Your life was headed in one direction and suddenly, *zowie!* Things are going to change. Your entire life will be different because of your parents' divorce.

But none of these changes is intentionally designed to hurt you. Your parents still love you, even if their love is hidden now behind their anger and hurt. These changes of house and school are basically neutral—what they make of you depends on what you make of them.

YOUR NEW HOUSE

Depending upon the details of your parents' divorce settlement and custody arrangements, you may have to move to a new house or apartment. Often couples who split property have to sell the family house so they can divide the proceeds fairly. Gone will be the family home with its memories. This could be a good thing—after all, the old place won't be around to remind you of bad memories of your parents' difficulties. If you have a lot of happy memories in your house, well, you can take happy memories anywhere.

If you must move into a new neighborhood or even a new state, try to see this opportunity as a fresh start. You'll be making new friends and meeting new people. Leave the unpleasant memories of the past behind.

A friend of mine told me a story about an old-timer who sat on his front porch at the outskirts of town. A family drove by and stopped to talk for a few minutes. "Hey, fella, what's the town ahead like?" the husband asked the old man.

"Depends," the grizzled man replied. "What was the town like where you're from?"

"Terrible," answered the wife. "The schools were terrible, everything's crowded, and the people were snobbish and un-friendly." The old-timer nodded. "Same thing on up ahead," he said simply. The family got back into their car and drove into town, where they found that things were just as the old man had said.

A second family drove up after a while and got out to stretch their legs. "Hey, fella, what's the town ahead like?" the husband asked the old man.

"Depends," the man replied, casually chewing on a straw. "What was the town like where you're from?"

"It was wonderful," answered the wife. "We hated to leave. The schools were great, the people were friendly, and the place was always busy with something to do."

The old-timer nodded. "Same thing on up ahead," he said

simply. The family got back into their car and drove on into town, where they found that things were just as the old man had said.

The moral of the story? What you make of a new place depends upon your attitude. If you go into a new situation expecting good things, you're likely to find them. If you go to a new place with negative attitudes and expecting the worst, you'll find that, too.

A NEW SCHOOL

Because of the changes in your address or your family's financial situation, you may have to transfer to a new school. Not only will you be the "new kid on the block," you will also be the kid who lives with only one parent. Don't worry. There are lots of kids who live with only one parent.

Remember Daniel from *The Karate Kid?* Daniel lived with his single-parent mom, he moved to a new apartment and a new school, and he just couldn't seem to fit in anywhere. He was a nice kid, but he didn't have a car, he didn't have a father, and he didn't live in the best neighborhood. Even his karate wasn't what he wished it was.

Daniel's old friends were gone. His father was gone. His new friend abandoned him after Daniel was beaten up by a rich bully. His mother was busy working. Daniel's only friend was an elderly Japanese custodian who never said more than five words at a time. But because Daniel learned to trust the wisdom of the old man, he came out a winner.

Sometimes you may feel like Daniel—beaten, disliked, underprivileged, and ignored. Hang in there! If you learn to trust the wisdom of God, you'll come out a winner, too.

A word of caution: If you change addresses or schools, don't surrender to the temptation to make such a fresh start that you give up your ideals and standards just to fit into a popular group. Some kids move into a new neighborhood and decide they are going to be the exact opposite of what they were in their old schools. They begin to hang out with the kids who party all the time, and they do things they would never have done before.

Don't be so desperate for friends that you do things you know are wrong. It doesn't take any backbone or character to "go with the flow." A chameleon blends into whatever background he's in, but he is also the most cowardly animal on the face of the earth. When he hears a footstep approaching, he skitters off like the wind, as fast as his four timid legs can carry him. Chameleons aren't brave. It doesn't take any courage to blend into the crowd. Ben Jonson once said, "He knows not his own strength that hath not met adversity." In other words, you'll find out how strong you are when you go through tough times.

You see, God doesn't allow tough times to come your way so he can test you. God already knows how strong you are! God allows tough times to come so that *you* can find out how strong you are. Like the karate kid, you'll discover your own strength when you meet adversity.

YOUR CHANGING FINANCIAL SITUATION

Have you been thinking about getting a job to help out financially? Do you dream of the day you can buy your mom a new car or even a house? You may have noticed she doesn't have the nice things other mothers have.

Divorce seems to bring the financial problems most families have into sharper focus. Before the divorce your family may have been supported by one or two paychecks, but now there may be only one or none. Some mothers go on welfare after a divorce. Many kids find that the paycheck from their part-time job can't be spent on records and clothes anymore. Instead that hard-earned money is needed for buying groceries or for a college fund.

The average standard of living for a divorced woman and her children goes down 73 percent in the first year after a divorce while her husband's standard of living goes up 42 percent. When alimony is awarded, it is usually only about $350 a month for two years. Child support is an average of $200 a month for two children, and 60 percent of divorced fathers fail to support their children at all. That is far less than half of the cost of raising children.[1]

More than 80 percent of children whose parents have divorced live with their mothers; the 1985 average income for such single-parent families with children from the age of twelve through seventeen was $15,249, compared to $27,600 for families that had a father as the head.[2]

Maybe you're not into statistics, but they should help you understand why your mother is suddenly complaining about bills and fussing at you for forgetting to turn off the lights or leaving the refrigerator door open. If she is a single mother, her income has probably changed dramatically since the divorce. Money is tighter now, and your mother needs your understanding.

If finances are tight in your family, ask your mom or dad what you can do to help. Perhaps you and your parent will want to go over the family budget together. Finances put a lot of pressure on adults, so try to be more understanding the next time your mom says, "We can't afford it."

Maybe your biggest area of financial frustration is the area of clothing—you can't afford to wear the "right" kind of clothes. A few years ago I interviewed Dr. Benjamin Carson, a renowned pediatric neurosurgeon at Johns Hopkins Hospital in Baltimore. Dr. Carson's parents divorced when he was eight years old, and he and his brother were raised by their mother.

Once, Dr. Carson remembers, he began following a certain crowd and felt a keen pressure to dress the way everyone else did. "There was a great emphasis on clothing," he says, chuckling, "particularly on Italian-knit shirts. I was always telling my mother I had to have these things, that they were the most important things in life. Naturally, she was disappointed. So one day she said, 'Benji, I'm going to turn all the money over to you. You pay the bills, buy the food, and take care of everything. With the money left over, you can buy all the Italian-knit shirts you want.'

"I was thrilled. But after I got through allocating all the funds, there was nothing left; so I never asked for a shirt again. I started to recognize that following the crowd wasn't so important after all."

Dr. Carson's favorite words of wisdom were passed on to him from his mother: "Don't make excuses for yourself," he says. "Everybody has obstacles in life, no matter where they come from, and the determinant of success is how one faces those obstacles. If you see them as a containing wall, you won't go any farther, and you will allow them to define your ability. But if you see them as hurdles, you can jump over them and get good at jumping over them. Soon you'll be looking for others to jump over, and nothing can stop you."[3]

YOUR PARENTS MAY CHANGE

Not only might your address, your school, and your financial situation change, but even your parents may change before your eyes. Some adults are devastated by divorce. Others learn something from the experience and are stronger because they went through it.

Your parents may also be changing because of what's popularly known as a "mid-life crisis." Some people claim this condition as a cop-out when they don't want to face their problems, but other adults are genuinely bothered when they realize they have already lived more than half of their life. *What have I done with my life?* your parent may be wondering. *I'm forty years old, and I have never accomplished any of my personal dreams.*

Maybe this restless and melancholy condition was part of the reason your parents' marriage broke up. Maybe your father or mother walked out to search for a "new beginning" instead of dealing with the life they had already established. Mid-life crisis is a poor excuse and a lousy way to end a marriage, but your parent may be going through it.

YOUR FAMILY WILL CHANGE

Divorce brings the biggest change to your family unit. In a divorce your family is suddenly split like the amoebas you've watched under the microscope in biology class. What was one unit suddenly becomes two. Perhaps you will be separated from your brothers and sisters. You will be separated from one parent for days, weeks, or months at a time. The divorce may even separate you from your pets—sometimes people argue bitterly in court over who gets custody of the dog!

Your role in the family may change. You may find yourself behaving more like your parent's protector than her child. Your parent may give you unusual independence or begin to cling to you. None of these changes are unusual, and they will usually pass.

Always remember that although the family unit you have known will no longer exist as a whole, you will not lose the people you love. You will still have a mother and father, though you may not see them as often as you once did.

Your home may not have been perfect, but before the divorce there probably were times when you gathered around the table, and for a moment, at least, your family seemed happy and united like a winning team.

After the divorce certain things may improve, but even on the best days your family will not look like a united team. Someone will be missing. Does that mean your family will always feel like a mutation or a freak of nature?

No. Things will be different, yes, but if you were a joyful person before the divorce, you can be a joyful person again. It will take time and effort, but you can overcome the anxieties and fears that are bound to surface when you are faced with the changes divorce can bring.

You may feel like an oddball for a while, but you are not different from your friends. They may or may not be from divorced homes, but you are a person with likes and dislikes, abilities and weaknesses, intelligence and skills just like they are. The person you are does not have to change.

There are others your age who are also going through family divorces. Like you, they're learning to cope with changes in their family unit. Like you, they're searching for the security they once took for granted. Like you, they're trying to make sense of adult mistakes in an adult world.

One girl once told me that her family was like a beautiful ceramic bowl that shattered during the divorce. She was left with only pieces.

You can look at divorce from that perspective, but you can also consider that your family was like a large diamond in the hands of God. Sure, divorce shattered the diamond. It will never be as large as it was before, but God can take each little diamond piece and polish it into a beautiful gem. Best of all, those diamond pieces can be refitted into another setting, just as you can become part of another family through your parent's remarriage or a marriage of your own. You are a diamond in the rough, and you can still shine in beauty!

Best of all, God, the master diamond cutter, absolutely never, *ever* changes.

FOR MEMORIZATION AND MEDITATION

Hebrews 13:5-6, 8

"Keep your lives free from the love of money and be content with what you have, because God has said, 'Never will I leave you; never will I forsake you.' So we say with confidence, 'The Lord is my helper; I will not be afraid. What can man do to me?' . . . Jesus Christ is the same yesterday and today and forever."

James 1:17

"Every good and perfect gift is from above, coming down from the Father of the heavenly lights, who does not change like shifting shadows."

CHAPTER SIX
Alanna Dansk

T he phone rang, and I grabbed it before Kenyon. Dorian was supposed to call, and if some girl was calling Kenyon, the line would be tied up for an hour.

"Hello," I said, hoping to hear Dorian's voice.

"Hey, kiddo," my dad answered. "You must have been expecting me to call. Did your mom tell you I was picking you and Kenyon up for dinner tonight?"

I glanced toward the front door, but Mom hadn't come in yet from her new job. "No, she didn't. Tonight, Dad? I've got a load of homework to do."

"That's OK, I won't keep you long. Is Kenyon there, too? I want to take both of you out for dinner and show you my new apartment."

The memory of our last disastrous dinner thrust itself into my mind, and I had to bite my tongue to keep from saying, "Forget it, Dad. Just leave us alone." I couldn't say that. After all, Daniel Davis is my father, and despite everything he's done, I still love him.

"OK, Dad. What time do you want to pick us up?"

"Six o'clock. You guys be ready, OK?"

"OK."

I hung up the phone and went upstairs to tell Kenyon the news.

At six o'clock sharp Dad's black BMW pulled into the driveway and honked. "He's here," I announced to Kenyon. "Let's see if we can actually get through dinner without a fight, OK?"

"OK with me," Kenyon answered, grabbing his jacket from the back of a chair. "As long as he doesn't start anything. He knows how I feel about him."

I shook my head and locked the front door, feeling really strange and confused. I loved my dad, but I hated what he did to my mother; I loved my mother, too, but a tiny part of me hated whatever she did that helped kill their marriage.

Dad got out of the car and opened the rear door as Kenyon and I approached. "You two look good," he said, smiling casually. "I hope you're hungry. We're taking you to the Aussie Steak House, so you'll need an appetite."

"We?" I asked, peering into the car. "Who's with you?"

The dark-tinted front window slid smoothly down. "Hello, you two. I'm Alanna Dansk," a smooth voice offered. "It's a pleasure to meet you at last."

I felt as though someone had thrown a bucket of ice water over me. What was that woman doing here? Why had my father brought the witch along?

I felt a hand at my back, and Kenyon prodded me. "Get into the car, Kels," he said, ignoring Alanna. "I'm starving."

No one said much of anything at dinner. Alanna Dansk, her big blue eyes shining in the candlelight, ate little and looked around a lot. I kept my eyes mostly down on my plate as I pushed my food around with my fork. Ever since Alanna had introduced herself, I hadn't felt like eating. I didn't know if I'd ever feel like eating again.

Kenyon ate like a horse, though, and concentrated on his food, grunting occasional answers to Dad's polite questions about the school's football team. Dad seemed polite and casually at ease, eating with gusto and nodding frequently to Alanna.

When Alanna wasn't looking, I sneaked peeks at her. She was a beautiful woman, though much too young for Dad, I thought. She was wearing black leather jeans, which would have looked wrong on anyone else, and a slinky turquoise blouse that looked like silk. Her nails were perfectly manicured, her jewelry small and elegant, and her blonde hair was artfully swept back in a French twist.

"Alanna is a corporate vice president of the Peabody Corporation," I heard Dad explain. There was a touch of pride in his voice as he added, "She earned an MBA at Harvard."

"What's an MBA?" Kenyon asked, his mouth full of fried onions.

Dad chose to overlook Kenyon's terrible manners and patiently explained, "A master's degree in business administration."

I wanted to throw up. My mother never even went to college because she and Dad had married the year after Mom graduated from high school. Mom could have gone to college and earned an MBA, too, if she hadn't stayed home to raise Dad's kids and take care of his house.

Dad interrupted my thoughts. "You're very quiet tonight, Kels. Don't you think it would be polite to join in the conversation?"

I forced myself to swallow the piece of bread I'd been chewing. "Um, so what else do you do, Alanna?" I asked, without much enthusiasm.

Alanna beamed like she'd just won the Miss Universe contest. "Oh, nothing much. I work about twelve hours a day, go to the gym, and eat out a lot. Before Danny came along . . . ," she began and gave my dad an aren't-you-special smile, "I didn't do anything exciting. Now we're doing something practically every night."

"Oh, you did plenty, believe me," Dad answered, slipping his arm around Alanna. "I can't keep up with you even now."

"You do just fine," Alanna answered.

I let my fork clatter onto my plate. I wanted to throw up.

It was bad enough that Dad had asked us out with the woman who had destroyed our home, but apparently he expected me and Kenyon to actually *be nice* to her. That was asking too much.

~~~~~~~~~~~~~~~~

The house was still dark when Dad and Alanna brought us home. That meant Mom was still working at her new job in the law office. "I guess you two can let yourselves in," Dad said, putting the car in park. "Thanks for coming along. I wanted to spend some time with you, and I wanted you to meet Alanna, too."

"Thanks, Dad," I answered, more from polite habit than from sincerity. I felt like I was thanking one of the neighbors for bringing me home. I opened the car door and slid out of the backseat.

"Do you have your key?" Alanna called, trying too hard to be helpful.

"We have everything we need," Kenyon yelled back. He passed me on the sidewalk and whispered as he walked by, "Hurry up, Kels, and get your key out. I don't want to be in that woman's sight for one more minute."

I giggled in relief and fished my key out of my purse. Within two minutes we were safely inside our own house, and soon we heard the roar of Dad's car as it sped away.

"Can you believe he brought that woman to dinner?" I asked, snapping on the light in the living room. "He actually wants us to like her!"

"I wouldn't put anything past him," Kenyon answered, falling onto the couch. "He's terrible! I'm just glad Mom wasn't here to see that bimbo."

"Do you really think he's terrible?" I asked, sinking into a wing chair. "I mean, I don't like what he's done, but maybe Mom did something that drove him to it, you know? We don't really know what happened between them."

"I know he's been sneaking out for some time," Kenyon answered, looking over me. "Dad's had girlfriends for years. Some of them Mom knew about, some she didn't. But I know he put her through all kinds of grief, and I'm glad it's all going to be over. When they're divorced, Dad can run around and cheat on Alanna Dansk all he wants to. I won't care!"

I shook my head. "I guess I'm glad Mom won't have to worry about that anymore, but then I feel so guilty! What if Mom doesn't work out at her new job? What if she gets fired? I didn't tell you this, but the other night after her first day, she came home and cried for an hour in her room. She's under a lot of stress, and none of this would be happening if Mom and Dad were still together."

Kenyon clapped his hands over his ears. "I don't care. I'm glad they're divorcing. Mom will do OK. Dad will get what he deserves. And we'll be fine, Kelsey, just you wait and see."

~~~~~~~~~~~~~~

I think I'm going to take one of our family photograph albums when we visit Dad this weekend. Taking the old tattered album with its photographs of fun times won't be the most subtle thing I could do, but I don't know what else might knock some sense into my father's head.

Over the past few weeks my feelings have changed as rapidly as the faces of the people who keep tramping through our house with the real-estate man. One day I hate my father, the next day I miss him so much I can't stop crying. Sometimes I feel like I don't care if I never see him again, then I go down into the paneled room that used to be his office and smile at the plaques he left behind. He's so smart, my dad! I'm so proud of him! Then I think of him cuddling with Alanna Dansk, and I want to rip those plaques off the wall and tear the room apart.

Kenyon doesn't say much of anything to anyone. When we were younger, I really felt close to Kenyon, almost like he was a part of me. Mom always said we had "twin telepathy" and knew what the other was thinking because we had spent all that time in the womb together. But lately Kenyon has become a blank. I know he's angry, and nothing I say softens the wall he's built around his heart. Whenever Mom or I try to talk to him, Kenyon prickles like a porcupine.

I don't know what he'll do this weekend. It's our first official custodial weekend with Dad, the first of a long line of endless every-other-weekends with our father. Dad promised that we'd eat pizza and go out on the boat, and all that sounds like fun. If we get Dad in a good mood, I figure I could whip out the old photograph album, and just maybe he'll come around and realize what a good thing he's messing up. Then he'll come home, Kenyon will be normal again, and Mom can stop working twelve hours a day. Everything depends on this weekend.

D-I-V-O-R-C-E: IS THAT HOW YOU SPELL RELIEF?

Maybe you feel like Kenyon—the divorce of your parents actually brought you a feeling of relief. *I'm glad,* you may have thought. *Now I won't have to put up with their fighting . . . or drinking . . . or running around. . . .*

Courtney was eleven when her parents divorced, and she was hurt, angry, confused, and *relieved* when it was all over. Her dad drank a lot and had several affairs with other women. Courtney was happy when he finally left the house for good.

Twelve-year-old Troy felt tremendous relief when his mother divorced his father. They fought all the time, Troy remembers, and his father drank and abused his mother. One time Troy ran to the police for help. He says he wishes his mother had never married his father and frankly admits, "I hate him."

Maybe one of your parents divorced the other for "the good of the children." Years ago many people believed it was better for the kids if the family stuck together at all cost, but more people today think that miserable parents create miserable kids. So whether for good or bad, fewer parents today are willing to stay together for the sake of their kids. Divorce is so commonly accepted that many kids want their parents to get a divorce. These kids can't wait to grow up and get out of an unhappy home.

If one of your parents was abusive or an alcoholic, you may be happier after the separation. You may not be upset by the divorce. You may be relieved, and with your relief may come a feeling of guilt. Are you *supposed* to be happy when your family splits up?

IF YOUR HOME WAS A NIGHTMARE

If your parents' marriage was very unhealthy and unhappy, it's possible that you were more alert to family problems than your parents were. You know what a family should be like because you've seen the "normal" homes of your friends. You've watched *Cosby* where two strong parents managed to take care of five kids and still love each other. If even fake families on television can solve a problem each week and still get along, why can't yours?

Maybe your father is an abusive alcoholic. When he comes home drunk, he thinks nothing of slapping your mom as the mood strikes him. You and your brothers and sisters have learned to stay out of his way, but your mother has no place to run.

"Mom," you want to tell her, "you should get out of this. This is not right."

You can't bring friends to your house because life is just too unpredictable. Will your dad be there? Will he be sane or raving mad? Will your mother look OK, or will she have a bruise on her cheek?

You'd give anything for your parents to separate. You've talked to your school counselor, maybe you've even called the police. You've looked through your dad's car for some kind of evidence that might convince your mom to leave him. You can't stand to watch him hurt her. He is destroying your mother physically, mentally, and socially, and you love her too much to let it continue.

When the divorce finally comes, you may be relieved, but you might feel a bit guilty because you participated in the breakup of your own home. As time passes, you may forget just how awful those drunken nights were and only remember the good things about having your mother and father together. It wasn't *always* bad. Perhaps your relief will fade and your guilt will begin to grow. Your mind may try to cover the painful memories and amplify the pleasant ones.

You may feel terrible if your mother does not handle the divorce well. If your mom has no career skills and cannot earn enough money to support herself and you kids, your guilt may grow. If she cries from loneliness and tells you that she still loves your father, you may feel like a traitor.

If you do, don't wallow in guilt; instead, face the truth. Remember what life was like under the tyranny of this man whose heart was filled with sin. Unless through a miracle he turns to Jesus

Christ and finds a new life, he probably will not change. Don't hate your father—pray for him.

Your mother needs prayer, too, because she was under domination so severe that she was damaged emotionally and spiritually. Her self-esteem is low; she may have been browbeaten by words and fists for years. You cannot expect her to simply pick up a briefcase and march out of the house with mature, capable confidence. She will need time to heal.

You and your siblings will need time to recover. Did you know that children who see their parents frequently argue or fight get lower grades in school? It's true. They also pick up their parents' patterns of conflict resolution.[1] In other words, if you've seen your parents resort to violence to end an argument or make a point, you may feel the only way to settle a conflict is to punch someone. Time, understanding, and godly leadership will help you learn new ways to resolve difficulties.

WHERE CAN YOU GET HELP?

If your father was abusive and your mother is emotionally damaged, where can you and your brothers and/or sisters get help? Try your local church.

If your mother was abused, she will be able to find healing through a relationship with Jesus Christ. She'll be able to fellowship with other Christians at church. You and your brothers and sisters need to find friends and adults who care about you and can guide you through life. It's important to have someone mature and confident to look up to, someone who knows some of the answers to life's questions.

I don't know what you've heard, but churches are neither full of hypocrites nor full of perfect people. Churches are made up of people just like you and me, people who make mistakes. There are divorced people in churches, too, and people whose lives have been touched by alcoholism, drugs, and abuse. But people in churches are learning to let Jesus Christ heal those past hurts.

Somewhere in your area there is a church with a good youth program and a pastor who preaches the truth from the Bible. Somewhere there are men and women who will care about you. There are loving homes where men don't drink and women don't beat their children and yell all day. You can have a home like that—if not now, then one day when you establish your own home. The church can help you learn how to do it.

LOOK FOR A HERO

Along with finding help at church, you can also find help in other families. My friend Cody Clark remembers how he looked for love when he was younger. "I cannot tell you how many parents have pulled me into their families," he says. "I felt like I was so different because even my friends who had divorced families knew where their fathers were, but I did not. I never knew where my father was or if I looked like him. But I attached myself to people—church was my first outlet. I'd think, *Gee, I'd really like to be like him or do what he's doing.*

"My mom allowed me to be involved in this, and she never said she didn't want me out with those people. That's why I was able to pick my role models. Some of the adults that played the role of father are still around. I loved them, I needed them. I emulated them and wanted to grow up and be like them."

Somewhere, maybe in church or maybe at school, there is someone older who can provide the missing element in your life. Look for a hero, but guard yourself carefully. Unfortunately, there are people who would take advantage of you for their own selfish desires, so look for a hero who will guide you, not someone who will use you.

ONE FINAL WORD

While you're looking for help and healing, don't discard your parents. Don't let your hurt and anger turn into bitter hate. God tells us to honor our parents, so even if you don't respect them at this time in your life, don't do anything to ridicule or belittle your mom or dad. Pray for them. Encourage them. And wait patiently for God to work in their lives.

FOR MEMORIZATION AND MEDITATION

Luke 6:37
"Do not judge, and you will not be judged. Do not condemn, and you will not be condemned. Forgive, and you will be forgiven."

Ephesians 6:1-3
"Children, obey your parents in the Lord, for this is right. 'Honor your father and mother'—which is the first commandment with a promise—'that it may go well with you and that you may enjoy long life on the earth.'"

Fishing

T he photograph album stayed in my backpack. It wasn't that I didn't get a chance to bring it out, it was simply that I was having too good a time to risk putting my plan into action. I've never seen my dad so relaxed.

On the boat, my dad was calm and easygoing, baiting my hook and helping me cast my rod into the choppy waters of the Atlantic. Kenyon handled his rod expertly and didn't need or ask for help, and Dad seemed to sense that Kenyon wasn't ready or willing to talk. So Dad and I talked and laughed and had a great time, the best time I have ever had with my father.

It was almost like he was someone else's dad. He was charming and handsome and caring. He asked about school, he joked about my windblown hair, and reached out to steady me when a rogue wave hit the boat and would have sent me flying across the deck. It was as though he didn't have a care in the world, and I wondered why he had always seemed so different at home. Was he standoffish at home because of the pressure between him and Mom? All those hours he spent in his office at home—did he go to that room to work, or because it was the one room where he could get away from Mom?

Dad went to the wheel of the boat to drive us to another inlet, and I stared down at the foamy waters that churned at the back of the boat. It seemed disloyal to think bad thoughts about my mother. After all, Dad was the one who had a girlfriend. He was the one who left home. My mom was suffering and all because of him. Or was it really all his fault?

"Dad," I called above the roar of the outboard motor and the wind in my ears, "did you really love Mom?"

My father shifted into low gear abruptly and squinted over at me. Kenyon's head jerked back in surprise, and he turned to look at me, too.

"Well, yes, I loved her very much," Dad answered, cutting the boat's motor. He turned to face me and folded his hands. "When we were first married, I thought nothing would ever come between us."

"What did?" Kenyon asked, his voice unusually gruff.

"Time, I think," Dad answered, leaning back in his seat. "That and a lack of effort. I got caught up in my career, your mom got involved in you kids, her job, and the PTA. We spent all our time on other things, and when we did get together, all we did was complain to each other. When we grew tired of fighting and complaining, there was only silence left between us."

I knew about the silence. That part I remembered. I felt the sting of tears in my eyes, so I turned my face toward the water.

"I failed in my marriage," Dad said simply. "And I've decided that whatever else I do, I'm not going to fail at being your dad. I love you both, and I'm going to spend the time it takes to be a good dad to both of you."

I let my pole drop to the deck of the boat and rushed to the security of my father's arms. He patted my shoulder awkwardly and I cried, letting all the tears of the past weeks come pouring out. When I had finished crying, my father kissed my forehead, and I relaxed in his embrace.

Kenyon, I noticed, was still hanging on to his fishing rod, his face out to sea.

~~~~~~~~~~~~~~~~

We walked into a hailstorm of questions when we got home on Sunday afternoon. "Where did you go?" Mom asked, sinking onto a bar stool as Kenyon and I helped ourselves to snacks in the kitchen. "What'd you do? I suppose he brought that woman along."

"No, he didn't," I said firmly, pouring myself a glass of lemonade. "We went fishing on the boat on Saturday, and we went to church together this morning. It was Dad's idea."

"You went to our church?" Mom's eyes widened. "Why, I haven't been able to hold my head up there! I can't believe your father went—what must people be thinking?"

I shrugged. "Dad thought it was a good idea."

Mom's worried eyes caught mine. "What else? Did that woman call? What does his new place look like? I suppose it's really nice. He'll get the nice place, and after we move, we'll be living in a dump."

"It's an OK place, nothing fancy," I answered, feeling a little irritated. The pleasurable glow of the weekend was quickly evaporating. Why was my mother being such a pain?

I drank my lemonade quickly and began to walk out of the kitchen, but Mom grabbed my sleeve. "I don't suppose you care what I did this weekend. I was off from work, you know, but I had to study all those computer manuals so I'll know how to work the word processor. I thought I'd go nuts by myself in this big house. It was just terrible, and here you two come back with sunburned faces from all your fun in the sun!"

"Sorry, Mom," I answered, pulling away. "I really want to go take a nap. I'll talk later, OK?"

Kenyon slipped past her, too, and together we hurried out of the kitchen. When we were around the corner, we both broke into a run and raced up the stairs before the questions could begin again.

THE GAMES PEOPLE PLAY

"The kids are with you all week, so I insist on seeing them over the holiday weekend."

"You can't have them if you're going to have that woman there, too. I will not have my kids associating with your so-called girlfriend!"

"It's none of your business who's over here when the kids are with me. I'm their father and I have rights, too. I'll see you in court before I'll let you win on this one!"

And on the games go. There are lots of different games with different rules. The "I'll take you to court" game and the "If the child support check is late you're in trouble" game are just a few that divorced parents play.

Kids play divorce games, too. There's the "I don't have to obey you because you're not my real mom" game and the "You don't love me anymore" game. The trouble with these games is that no one has any fun!

GOSSIP

Players: a mother, a father, and a child; can also be played by grandparents

Duration of game: The game continues until the more mature player realizes how harmful the game is.

Directions: One of the adults serves as the instigator and begins the game. She will say something bad, mean, or harmful about the absent parent to the child. (For instance, Mom could say, "Your father is such a jerk! He never could handle responsibility.") The child is expected to laugh, listen, or agree.

Consequences of game: The child could actually begin to believe the negative gossip, or he could begin to resent the instigator. Gossip is a very destructive game with serious consequences.

HIDE AND SEEK THE TRUTH

Players: usually played by adults

Directions: Parents automatically assume that kids are incapable of understanding why parents have divorced. The kids are simply told about the divorce. (For instance, "Daddy is moving out because we don't love each other anymore.") Kids are left to seek out the truth for themselves. As the kids grow older, parents ignore the divorce or dismiss it as something that happened a long time ago. The kids are never told the truth, and they will always wonder what happened.

Consequences of game: The children will hear rumors or make up their own stories about the divorce. In time, they will wonder if the divorce was somehow their fault. If the kids do not often see the noncustodial parent, they may assume that he or she simply didn't love them.

PITY PARTY

Age: any age parent or child

Number of players: usually played alone or with close family members

Directions: After the divorce, the primary player becomes depressed and takes the hurt and pain entirely upon himself.

Player mutters, "It's all my fault," and looks for little illogical things to explain the breakup. Player resolves never to be happy or married and says that only fools fall in love.

Results of game: a lifetime of depression, anxiety, and loneliness

THE PRICE IS RIGHT

Ages of players: usually played by adults

Object of the game: for the "buyer" to earn the title of "favorite parent"

Directions: When the kids visit the noncustodial parent, he or she must take them out and splurge over and above what the budget allows. Clothes, toys, trinkets, trips to amusement parks, a new car—whatever will make the kids say, "I love you the most!"

When the kids return home and display their prizes, the other parent will either feel guilty, angry, or go on a spending spree to outdo the first player.

Caution: Although this game sounds like a sure bet for kids, most budgets will eventually be "busted." The parent who initiated the game will quit, and the letdown will be severe. If the second parent is unable to compete with the first parent, he or she will be hurt very deeply.

I SPY

Ages: usually played by adults using children as the game pieces

Number of players: one parent, unlimited number of children

Directions: After the kid's visit to his mother or father, the other parent will ask a series of questions, which grow more and more pointed. For instance:

"How's your mom?"

"What's she doing this weekend while you're with me?"

"She must get pretty lonely without you there, right?"

"Is she seeing anyone now? Who is this guy, anyway?"

"Where did she meet him? How long has she known him? What does he do for a living?"

"Has he, uh, been hanging around a lot? Does he keep his toothbrush at the house?"

Consequences of game: Most kids grow tired of questioning and give shorter and shorter answers. Parents have a hard time realizing that they are no longer married and have no right to ask personal questions about the other parent.

RED ROVER, RED ROVER, SEND ME RIGHT OVER!

Ages: usually played by kids old enough to tell a judge where they'd like to live

Directions: If Mom says no or won't let her kid do something, the kid simply says, "I wish I lived with Dad!" (or vice versa). If that doesn't do the trick, the player states more firmly, "I want to go to court and tell the judge I want to move!" If Mom still doesn't give in to the kid's wishes, he pretends to call his father and arranges to move in.

Caution: Sooner or later parents wise up to this game. Don't resort to emotional blackmail.

FINDERS, KEEPERS; LOSERS, WEEPERS

Ages: usually played by kids of divorce

Directions: When the father or mother begins to date, the kids try to make their dating lives as difficult as possible. If the girlfriend calls, the kids don't take a message and conveniently "forget" to tell Dad about it. They tell Dad that his girlfriend isn't nearly as pretty as Mom and can't cook at all. They suggest that

Mom's boyfriend is "over the hill" or only interested in her because he wants someone to clean his house.

Kids who play this game know it's OK to have fun with a parent's date as long as their parent is not around, but the moment Mom or Dad appears, they become cool and disagreeable. This demonstrates how much the third party upsets kids and may drive a wedge between parents and their dates.

Consequences: It won't take long for parents to figure this game out, and playing this game only builds a wall between kids and adults who really care about them.

MONOPOLIZE

Number of players: usually three or more, one of whom is a new stepparent

Directions: This game is begun by at least one of the children. The kid acts up in front of the stepparent, hoping his other parent will step in and defend him. If the parent does, the kid scores a minor victory. He is already chiseling away at the new marriage.

Next, the kid should let his grades slip. He also should do various things to try the stepparent's patience, like lingering in the shower so the stepparent is late for work. The wedge between parent and stepparent will grow deeper.

The kid scores a major victory if the stepparent leaves home for a period of "cooling off." This is the kid's cue to make things perfect at home—cook the parent's favorite meal, help with the household chores, study like a maniac. He must drop subtle hints like, "Isn't it great being just the two of us again?" and drag out the family photo album to look at pictures of the family as it used to be.

Winning the game: The kid is supposedly successful if the stepparent leaves and the parent goes through *another* divorce. The parent will once again be hurt beyond measure and feel like a total failure. The kid will have the parent all to himself for a few years, but when he leaves home, the parent will have no one.

Caution: If this plan backfires, the kid could find himself being shipped off to live elsewhere, or the stepparent could call his bluff and let the kid know his actions are selfish and cruel. Any way you play this game, *you lose.*

BE AS REALISTIC AS YOU CAN BE

Divorce games aren't fun, and they're not helpful, either. People who play any of the above divorce games are trying to deny reality and create a situation that doesn't—and shouldn't—exist. If you try to see things clearly and realistically, you won't be tempted to play divorce games.

It's not easy to be realistic about your parents' divorce. Kelsey was having that problem in this chapter—she wanted to blame her dad, yet she still wanted to love him. She wanted to defend her mother, but she also wondered what her mother had done to help the marriage fail.

Recently I talked to Samantha about her father. Samantha lives with her mother and has been having problems with her mom, so she has shifted blame—for nearly everything—onto her mother. It's easy to see that Sam really loves her father, even though she sees him only on weekends and a few holidays. He's unemployed and behind on his child-support payments, but Sam loves him so much she supports him aggressively.

"He's always making promises to my brothers and me that he can't fulfill," she says, "but we've just learned to overlook his promises. He says if he won a million dollars from the lottery, he would go to court and get custody of us. He'd also pay Mom the child support he owes. He'd send us to college. He says Mom doesn't know how it feels to just visit us two or three hours on weekends and holidays."

Sam told me about the years when her parents were married. When he was employed, her dad spent all his money on alcohol, forcing her mother to work two jobs. Between the two jobs and keeping house, she never saw her kids.

"Samantha, can't you see that your mother *does* know how it feels to never see her kids?" I asked her. "Don't you think that maybe your dad is not giving you a very realistic picture?"

Sam nodded her head thoughtfully, then shook it, dismissing the thought. "I don't like to think about reality. I like to think of my parents in my own way. They are both good people, and I love them."

It's OK to love both parents, in fact, it's *great* if you do. If you can't be realistic now, don't worry about it. In time, you'll be able to see things more clearly.

FOR MEMORIZATION AND MEDITATION

Job 11:18
"You will be secure, because there is hope; you will look about you and take your rest in safety."

Psalm 112:1, 7
"Blessed is the man who fears the Lord. . . . He will have no fear of bad news; his heart is steadfast, trusting in the Lord."

Proverbs 3:24
"When you lie down, you will not be afraid; when you lie down, your sleep will be sweet."

The Ugly, Muddy Hole

I think I'm ruined for life," I confided to Dorian as we lounged on her bed and looked at magazines.

"Why?" she asked, flipping her hair over her shoulder. "Just because you're peeling from that horrible sunburn? One burn won't give you cancer, you know."

"No," I answered, laughing. "It's not that. It's just that since my parents are getting divorced, I don't think I'll ever be able to get married myself." Dorian's smile evaporated, and we got really serious. I felt tears welling up in my eyes, and I pointed to a picture of a girl in jeans, trying to change the subject. "Those jeans are really cool," I blubbered, not able to keep the tears inside.

Dorian didn't say anything, but just laid her arm across my shoulders and let me cry. Finally she reached out and handed me a box of tissues. "You're not ruined for life," she said, pausing so I could blow my nose. "You're just going to have to be careful when you get married, that's all. You'll have to make sure that you're doing what's right."

"My dad says he loved Mom when they got married," I told her. "But somehow they stopped spending time together, and they just didn't have anything in common anymore."

"Then you'll spend *lots* of time with your husband,"

Dorian said firmly. "And you'll be careful to keep things in common. I mean, you'd like to spend more time right now with Jason, wouldn't you?"

I stopped sniffling. Jason, the wonderful guy of my dreams, hadn't been in my dreams much lately. Who had time for dreaming? Still, if we were really going together, and if he were my husband— "Yeah," I told Dorian. "I'd make time for Jason. In fact, I'd make time for Jason right now if he came through your door!"

"Me, too," Dorian added, and when I gave her a funny look, she corrected herself quickly. "I mean, I'd make time for my boyfriend, whoever he was. I'm not saying I like Jason. He's yours."

I sighed in relief, then made a face. "What do you mean, he's mine? The guy hardly knows I exist!"

Dorian giggled. "Wouldn't it be great if there really was such a thing as a love potion? You could stir it into some-body's drink, and *wham!* He'd be out of his gourd, crazy for you."

"Instant love," I snorted. "Sure, that'd be great—as long as the stuff tasted like chocolate."

Dorian laughed, then wrapped a strand of hair around her finger and began to twirl it slowly. I know her well enough to know that she was thinking, so I just let her think for a minute.

"You know, I've been thinking . . . ," she said, and I laughed.

"What, O thoughtful one?"

She smacked me on the arm. "Stop it. Really. I'm serious. I was thinking about love. What is it, really? I mean, what makes a guy love a girl, and what keeps old people together for hundreds of years?"

"I dunno." I rested my chin on my hands and studied the

lines in her bedspread. "I guess it's chemistry. You see some-body, then *zowie!* You're hooked."

"That's not love—that's infatuation," Dorian answered in her firmest no-nonsense voice. "You can be infatuated with a cartoon, for heaven's sake, or some movie character that's not even real. That's not love."

"Then what is?"

Dorian twirled her hair again. "I think maybe it's more like a decision you make. You say, 'I WILL LOVE THIS PERSON no matter what.' You know, like they do in the marriage vows—for better, for worse, in sickness and in health, and all that stuff."

"My parents didn't mean what they said, then," I an-swered. "Maybe no one really means it."

"I would mean it," Dorian answered. "I really would. And every day I would do whatever I had to do to keep love alive. Maybe love is like a plant, and you can't just stick it in the ground and expect it to grow. You have to give it sun and water and food and fresh air, or it'll die."

"A plant." I looked at Dorian like she'd flipped her lid. "Seriously, a plant? Like a big palm tree?"

"Yeah, that's good," Dorian answered, twirling her hair again. "And divorce is when the tree dies and the family gathers around and digs the tree out of the ground. You're hurting right now, Kels, because you've got nothing left but the big ugly hole in the ground."

I put my hand over my mouth and looked at the floor. Suddenly I wanted to cry and throw up at the same time. Dorian was absolutely right, though. Mom and Dad got a divorce and left me and Kenyon with nothing but an empty hole in our lives.

"You don't have to hurt forever, Kelsey," Dorian answered softly. "You can fill the hole with a love of your own. You can plant your own palm tree and feed it and water it and give it lots of sunshine. Then lots of little coconuts will fall to the ground, and new trees will grow right at the bottom of your tree."

I bit my lip and prayed that she was right.

~~~~~~~~~~

When I got home from Dorian's house, Kenyon was in the den watching TV, and Mom wasn't home. I made myself a peanut butter and raspberry-jelly sandwich at the kitchen counter and had taken three bites when Mom walked in.

"What is all this mess?" Mom shrieked. "Isn't it enough that I work all day without having to come home and start work all over again? You know how hard it has been for me lately, and you aren't doing a thing to make my life easier! We're supposed to be partners, but you aren't keeping your end of the bargain!"

While I stood there in shock, Mom burst into tears and ran to her room. Kenyon lifted his head from the couch and rolled his eyes. "Major heart attack!" he said, whistling. "What brought that on?"

My mouth was sticky with peanut butter, so I could only shake my head. The jar of peanut butter was out, so was the jelly, one dirty knife, and a few thousand bread crumbs, but I hadn't had time to clean up yet. What does Mom expect me to do? Is every little thing we do going to send her into a raving frenzy?

"It wasn't like this when Dad was here," I said once my mouth was free of food. "Mom wasn't nutsy. And we didn't have to do all the work around this place."

"Tell me about it," Kenyon said, peeking over the couch again. "Saturday I'm supposed to wash the car, vacuum the entire house, and take out the garbage."

I snorted. "That's kid stuff. I'm supposed to keep a grocery list, keep the place clean, and read Mom's mind. It's impossible!"

"That's not the worst part." Kenyon got off the couch, came into the kitchen, and leaned over the counter. "Dad's treating me like I'm his best friend or something," Kenyon said, his voice low. "I hate it, but he's been telling me stuff I don't want to hear. Private stuff about Mom and that Alanna woman." He shook his head in disgust.

I can't blame him for not wanting to hear that stuff. Yuck! What's going on? When did they stop being parents, and when did we stop being the kids?

YOU'RE NOT A CHILD ANYMORE, ARE YOU?

Thirteen-year-old Dana sat in front of me, nervously twisting her hands and trying to explain her relationship with her father since the divorce. "I act more like his mother or his best friend," she said. "I try to encourage him that everything will be OK. I send him little cards and call him on the days I don't get to see him. My parents are both good people, but I feel like I need to look out after my dad. He hasn't been able to hold a job, and he is always making promises he can't keep. My sisters and I have learned to just let him talk and say, 'Sure, Dad.'"

Perhaps you find yourself worrying about your mother. One day not long after the divorce she may have called you in and said, "It's going to be just you and me from now on. We're going to be partners and see this thing through to make it work."

After her parents' divorce, Stacy had to work hard to encourage her mother to survive. The woman was so upset that she refused to eat, and eleven-year-old Stacy became the "mother," coaxing, preparing food, trying anything to get her depressed mother to eat.

Dawn told us about her relationship with her mother: "My brothers hate my mother for the faults she has, but I'm her friend. If I hated her, she wouldn't be around—she would have moved away. She isn't all that bad. My brothers don't even want to go see her, but I call her and talk to her. I'm afraid if I'm not there for her, she'll move and I'll lose her."

If you are a girl, your mother may have begun to treat you more like a friend than a daughter. If you are a guy, you may have found yourself becoming a "substitute" man of the house. You automatically are expected to take more responsibility for the house: cleaning, repairing broken fixtures, taking out the garbage, maintaining the car.

WHEN EMOTIONAL CIRCUITS OVERLOAD

Remember when Kelsey's mom blew up over a peanut butter sandwich? What causes such outbursts? Stress. Pressure. Worry. Fear.

Your newly single parent is facing new fears and may feel like he or she is facing them all alone. Your parent desperately longs for someone she can count on, so she turns to her children for support. She may even lose perspective for a while.

Help your parent when you can. Give your dad some emotional space until the hurts heal, but don't feel guilty when he obviously overreacts to an innocent situation. Most important, don't get drawn into an emotional shouting match. You may both say things you really don't mean and later regret it. Wait until your emotions have calmed down, and then talk things out.

If your mom had an outburst like Kelsey's mom, the best thing you could do after the outburst is simply clean the counter and allow your mom to have a good cry in her room. When she is calm, apologize for the mess and say, "Mom, I was going to clean it up, but I had just finished making my sandwich. You must have had a hard day today." Show your support by offering to cook supper or clean the house. This will take some of the pressure off your mom.

What about the pressures on you? You're working through a divorce, too, not to mention school, exams, problems with friends, and boy/girl relationships. You may be worried about making decisions about your own future and finding your own identity. At this point in your life you cannot possibly assume total responsibility for your parent. You can, and should, help out where you are able, but you cannot take over your parent's role. You are the child, not the parent.

COMFORTABLE COMMUNICATION

Do you have a best friend who listens to all your problems and laughs with you when times are good? You probably know several people in whom you could confide, but what about your parents? Like you, your mom and dad have undergone major changes in their lives. They probably want to share their feelings with someone, but who can they turn to?

Perhaps they talk to you, and maybe you wish they wouldn't. Maybe your mom tells you things about your dad you'd rather not know, or maybe your dad tells you things about his new single life that make you uncomfortable. The older you are, the more likely it is that your parents will share "adult" discussions and observations with you, but somehow kids never feel comfortable knowing details about their parents' problems. Even thirty-year-old adults don't like to discuss one parent with the other because it's uncomfortable to be in the middle of a two-parent situation.

As a child of divorce, you may find yourself in the middle most of the time. When your mother complains about your father, you feel uncomfortable. If your father tells secrets about your mother, you wish you could close your ears or scream for him to stop.

We all want to be proud of our biological parents because they supplied the gene pool that molded us. It is natural that you should want to be proud of your father and mother. It's also natural that you should resent hearing negative comments about either of your parents—after all, you are part of them!

If your parents are having difficulty finding emotional healing a few months after the divorce, perhaps you could suggest that they see a counselor. Surprising as it may seem, many counselors say that a lot of divorced parents are sent to counseling at the suggestion of their children. Whether the counselor is a professional Christian counselor or your pastor, many people benefit from discussing their situation with a mature person who can offer a detached, unemotional perspective.

Remember, you are not responsible for healing your parents. Unless your parents heal emotionally, though, you will suffer along with them. So if you or your parents need a counselor to talk through their problems, find one without delay.

HOW'S YOUR MUDDY HOLE?

Somewhere down the road you'll begin to think about the day YOU will marry someone you love. Perhaps, after all that has happened, you feel like you'd rather not marry at all. Will a divorce, with all its pain and hurt, happen to you? All of the old anger and resentment may swell up inside, and you know the last thing you want is to have another home come apart. Is marriage worth the risk?

Think about this story: Thales was a Greek philosopher who lived about five hundred years before Christ. He never married or had children. Once he was talking with an esteemed lawyer friend, Solon, who teased him about not having children.

While they were talking, a messenger came from Athens, where Solon's family lived, and Solon eagerly asked for news.

"There is no news," said the messenger, "apart from the funeral of a great lawyer's son."

"Whose son was this?" Solon wanted to know.

"I cannot remember," replied the messenger, "but the father is a great man who is presently traveling abroad."

Solon began to fear that the man spoke of *his* son. "Was it the son of Solon?" he asked frantically.

"Yes, that was the name," the messenger replied.

When Solon fell apart and began to weep, Thales took him by the hand and gently said, "These things that can strike down even a man as resolute as you are the things that prevent me from marrying and raising a family."[1]

But Thales was wrong! You could go through life with his attitude, never risking love or emotion or taking a chance on another person because you're afraid of what might happen. But, as the song goes, "The one who won't be taken never learns to give, and the heart afraid of dying never learns to live."

Don't be like Thales. You have much to give.

CHOOSE TO MAKE YOUR MARRIAGE WORK

Dorian was right: Love is a choice. Many of the young people I interviewed expressed doubts about their future marriages, but just as many were determined to make their marriages *better* than their parents':

"I'm going to marry a *strong* Christian, and I'm going to make my marriage work."

"A divorce seems like an easy solution for the two parents, but the kids have to deal with it their whole lives. However, Christ can change hearts, circumstances, and even a seemingly impossible marriage. I'm going to do it God's way—'Hangeth thou in there' not 'getteth the heck out!'"

"I'm going to make sure I know the man well and make sure he loves me and God."

"I'm going to wait for the right person so we won't have to get divorced. I used to cry myself to sleep because I missed my dad so much. I wouldn't want that to happen to my kid."

As you grow older, learn all you can about Christian marriage and how men and women are supposed to relate to one another. Find a Christian couple with a good marriage and watch them closely to see how they relate to one another. Notice that they are best friends. Treat marriage as the most important endeavor and earthly relationship that you will ever undertake.

Which road are you going to choose? Depression or determination? Remember—you can take your personal muddy hole in the ground and fill it, or sit around all day and mourn the fact that nothing grows in your garden. It's your choice—it's up to you.

FOR MEMORIZATION AND MEDITATION

1 Corinthians 13:11

"When I was a child, I talked like a child, I thought like a child, I reasoned like a child. When I became a man, I put childish ways behind me."

James 1:2-4

"Consider it pure joy, my brothers, whenever you face trials of many kinds, because you know that the testing of your faith develops perseverance. Perseverance must finish its work so that you may be mature and complete, not lacking anything."

Storm Alert

The sun shone hot on our faces despite the November breeze as Kenyon and I walked home from the bus stop on Tuesday afternoon. When we reached our house, Kenyon stopped abruptly. "It's no big deal," I said, squinting at the pickup truck in the driveway. "It's probably just somebody who's here to look at the house."

"I don't think so," Kenyon answered, peering into the back of the truck. Inside were several sheets of plywood, half a dozen gallon-jugs of water, and several rolls of wide masking-tape.

"Hey kids, give me a hand, will you?" a voice called, and I whirled around to see Dad approaching from the house. He was sweating under his short-sleeved shirt, and he wore heavy cotton gloves.

"What are you doing?" I asked, more amazed that Dad was home than at his strange dress.

"Haven't you heard?" Dad smiled his lopsided smile, but his eyes were serious. "Hurricane Chad has formed out in the Atlantic, and they think it may be headed this way. I'm surprised you didn't hear about it in school today."

"A hurricane?" Kenyon's voice ended in an embarrassing squeak. He dropped his book bag on the lawn and reached for a sheet of plywood in the truck. "Can I give you a hand?"

"Sure." Dad smiled and grabbed the edge of a plywood sheet. "I'm hammering this plywood over the windows, and I brought some other supplies that are already in the house. Kels, why don't you bring in the water?"

"OK." I nodded and dropped my book bag next to Kenyon's. The hurricane could have my schoolbooks, I didn't care. But, miracle of miracles, the hurricane had brought my dad home. A sudden wave of thankfulness swept over me, and I bowed my head to pray. "Thanks, God. I didn't know you'd have to send a hurricane, but thanks for bringing Dad back."

~~~~~~~~~~~~

Mom had the television turned to the Weather Channel and the television weatherman kept repeating, "Hurricane Chad is currently moving through the Bahamas. Residents of Palm Beach County are currently under a hurricane watch. Evacuation notices have not yet been issued."

"Is it really going to come here?" I squealed. "How exciting! We've never had a hurricane actually come through here!"

"I don't think we want one," Kenyon answered, his eyes glued to the television map where a large red dot symbolized the approaching storm. "Remember all the damage that Hurricane Andrew did in south Florida? They're still rebuilding down there!"

"Let's see, I've filled your gas tank," Dad announced, coming into the room where we were all staring at the TV screen. "There are several working flashlights upstairs in the linen closet, and the radio in the kitchen has fresh batteries. Barbara, do you have a hand-held can opener and plenty of canned foods?"

At the sound of her name, Mom jerked her head away

from the television screen. "Yes, plenty of food," she said, cracking a wry smile. "We've even got propane in the grill, so if the power goes off, we'll barbecue outside."

"This isn't going to be a picnic," Dad answered, taking off his gloves. "I had enough plywood to do the big windows, but you'll have to tape the smaller windows. There's fresh drinking water in the jugs, but you should fill the bathtubs so you'll have water for washing dishes and flushing toilets."

"We'd better clean them first," I quipped, crinkling my nose. "Our bathtub is a mess."

"Get to it, then," Dad said. "Kenyon, give me a hand with the patio furniture. We can't leave anything outside that might blow through a window."

"Good grief," Kenyon grumbled good-naturedly, standing up, "do you think the wind can move the patio furniture?"

"The winds from Hurricane Andrew blew the paint off houses," Dad said, his face grim. "I'm not taking any chances with you guys. Barbara, get some sheets or something to cover the rug, and we'll bring in the outdoor furniture and any plants you've got out there."

From the kitchen, where I had gone to get the cleanser, I couldn't help smiling. It didn't matter that a hurricane was coming. All that mattered was that despite everything, Dad still cared about all of us. He had dropped his work and come riding to the rescue, and he was going to stay with us.

We were all together again in our house, working as a family. Maybe the divorce wouldn't ruin our lives after all.

~~~~~~~~~~~~

Waiting for a hurricane is really strange. You hear that it's coming, you can see it on the weather map, but outside the sun shines as bright as always. Then the winds pick up a little bit, and your stomach tightens because you know the storm is on its way.

We were under an official hurricane warning for nearly ten hours before the winds began to pick up. Mom, Kenyon, and I sat glued to the television screen, and Dad puttered around the house making sure everything was OK. At one point I heard him in his office talking to someone on the phone; a few minutes later he came into the living room and stood there for a minute watching us.

"I think you'll be OK," he said, and I jumped. Why did he say *you*? Wasn't he going to stay with us?

"It's only a category three hurricane, so the winds shouldn't be above 130 miles per hour," Dad said. "This house was built to stand up to winds of up to 150. But if the order for an evacuation comes, Barb, or if they declare it a category four hurricane, I want you all to get into the car and head out of town. Go to Orlando and take a hotel room." His eyes met Mom's. "Use the credit card, Barbara, and I'll pay the bills. I don't want anything to happen to you."

Mom nodded slowly, and I could see she wasn't surprised that he was leaving. What had happened? Just five minutes ago he was our dad, fixing our house and staying with us! How could he walk out on us just as the hurricane winds were beginning to blow?

"I'll be in touch as soon as I can," Dad said, grabbing his old tattered raincoat from the hall closet.

"Where will you be?" I asked, not wanting to hear the answer. Dad looked at me and seemed to hesitate before answering. "I'll be at Alanna's," he answered finally. His voice was low. "If you need me, you can try to call, but the phone lines will probably be out once the storm hits."

Then he turned and walked out the door. I couldn't believe it. I ran to the tiny window in the door and pressed my face to the glass as the rain began to fall outside, driving sheets of rain that pelted the door so forcefully I could feel the pressure from the inside.

"Kelsey, come away from the door," my mother called from the living room. "We're going to be in for a long night."

~~~~~~~~~~~~~~~~

When the power went out at about eight o'clock, Mom suggested that we go to bed. "Everything seems to be holding up all right," she said, eyeing the boarded-up windows warily. "Why don't we all get some sleep? If the power is out for a few days or if the water goes out, we'll have a lot of work to do tomorrow."

Kenyon and I climbed the stairs and listened to the wind roar around us. The power had gone off just after the man on the Weather Channel had announced that Hurricane Chad was headed for Palm Beach County, and the radio announcer just kept saying that Chad was on his way.

The wind seemed to almost scream as Kenyon and I stood outside our rooms. Kenyon looked at me, and I knew he was as scared as I was. "Can I get my blanket and sleep in your room?" I asked.

Kenyon nodded. When we were little, we used to sleep in the same room, but we hadn't done it in ages. Now, more than anything, I wanted to be with my brother.

Kenyon had the trundle bed pulled out by the time I came back with my pillow and blanket. I jumped on the trundle and curled up in a ball as the wind roared all around us. It sounded like a screeching demon outside tearing at the walls and roof.

But the walls seemed to hold. The window wasn't breaking. And the glow of Kenyon's flashlight shone on the ceiling, assuring us that everything was OK. I don't know how I did it, but I fell asleep.

~~~~~~~~~~~~~~~~

I didn't sleep for long. A loud tearing noise woke me up, and suddenly Kenyon grabbed at me and jerked me up from the trundle bed. Mom was there, too, screaming as the light from her flashlight bounced off the walls.

"The roof's coming off," she yelled above the noise that surrounded us. "Downstairs! Hurry!"

We stomped downstairs, and all I could think was that some giant named Chad had picked up the house and was shaking it up and down. Things were flying around inside, papers and books and pieces of pink insulation from the ceiling. Rain was everywhere; wind slapped my face and tugged at my blanket, but Kenyon and Mom were there, too, hurrying me down the stairs.

"The bathroom!" Kenyon yelled, steering me into the hall. "It's got pipes in the walls! We've got to stay in the bathroom!"

Mom pushed me through the bathroom doorway, Kenyon followed her, and suddenly we were in the darkness of our windowless bathroom. In the dim light of Mom's flashlight I could see water sloshing out of the filled bathtub. The entire house was shaking; the porcelain toilet lid jiggled and rattled as the house shook. One of the towel rods on the wall suddenly sprang out of the wall and clattered to the tile floor.

Mom thrust her flashlight into my hand. "Hold this, Kelsey!" she yelled. "Kenyon, help me hold the door!"

Together they braced their backs against the narrow bathroom door, and I closed the lid of the toilet seat and sat down, holding the light on Mom and Kenyon. Kenyon's face was frozen in fear, and Mom had a look of crazy desperation on her face. She glanced at me and then the flashlight and yelled again. "Save the battery! Keep the light off!" I could barely hear her above the noise, but I turned the light off, and we sat in total darkness as the house crumbled around us.

~~~~~~~~~~~~~~~

That night was an unending stretch of wind, water, and fear. I've never been so scared in my life—not even when I first thought about Mom and Dad getting a divorce. After all, when I found out about the divorce, I knew we were alive and that we'd keep on living somehow, just separately. But during that storm I wondered if we were all going to die. I wondered if the house would fall in and kill me, Mom, and Kenyon, and I worried about Dad, wherever he was. And worrying about dying is a lot worse than worrying about moving to a new house. Trust me.

Once the noise got so bad Mom started to scream. I don't even think she knew she was screaming, but I switched on the flashlight and saw that her eyes were wide, her mouth was open, and her body was tense as she kept pushing against the bathroom door. The wind blew and jostled her and Kenyon, at one point nearly knocking both of them over, but somehow they held it. Shingles from the roof blew in under the door, the tub actually detached from the wall and bounced toward us, and the sink cracked.

I think I screamed, too, during that time, but I don't remember. All I remember is thinking that I'd never be the same again, then I thought we were going to die. That's when I began to pray out loud, over and over, "God, save us. Please save us."

~~~~~~~~~~~~~~~

WILL DIVORCE RUIN YOUR LIFE?

Even though you may not have gone through a hurricane or a tornado, if you've gone through a divorce, you've been through a major storm. Hurricanes and tornadoes leave a trail of physical damage—wrecked houses, flipped cars, flooded streets. Divorce leaves invisible damage, but it can wreck lives, flip families, and flood your heart with grief. Both kinds of storms can change your life forever.

But the change can be for your good. In A.D. 399 St. Augustine said, "People travel to wonder at the height of mountains, at the huge waves of the sea, at the long courses of the rivers, at the vast compass of the ocean, at the circular motions of the stars—and they pass by themselves without wondering."[1]

You are a miracle! Just as you are, you are a wonderful creation! Eleanor Roosevelt once said, "No one can make you feel inferior without your consent." You should not give that permission to anyone, not even yourself. God made you, and as the saying goes, "God don't make no junk!"

But sometimes it's easy to forget that we are God's special creations when we're full of all the bad feelings that arise from a divorce. Maybe the divorce or separation has you feeling hateful, depressed, ugly, jealous, or angry. You don't feel like your old self, and you certainly don't feel like one of God's special creations!

Courtney is an exceptionally pretty girl. She has long, dark curly hair, a gorgeous natural tan, arresting blue-green eyes, and once was the life of every party. But two years ago her parents split up, and Courtney's natural enthusiasm slowly evaporated. She seems content now to sit on the sidelines and merely watch life and its activities.

She's not happy with things as they are. Courtney's parents fight over her, and she says she constantly feels hurt and confused. If she could change just one thing about her parents, she'd wish for her dad to be a Christian and her mom simply to be happy. Courtney's not only unhappy with her parents, she's disappointed in herself, too. What would Courtney change about herself?

Everything. "I want to be older, taller, have a better figure, and have longer hair. I want to be pretty."

Anyone would tell Courtney she is already pretty, and her friends frequently do. But Courtney's self-esteem has been so damaged she can't see her own worth. She doesn't understand that she is an attractive girl. Even if she weren't as beautiful on the outside, her sweet spirit would still shine forth and her inner beauty would light up her face.

Robin is another girl who has been hurt by divorce. "No one would tell me anything," she says. "I never understood *why* my parents divorced, and that drove me crazy." That sense of frustration has remained with her, even though her parents split up years ago. She is also frustrated about her appearance and her body. Unhappy with herself, Robin is usually unhappy with the world.

The parents of Jonathan Winters, the famous comedian, split up when he was seven. The other children teased him because he had no father.[2] To hide his own pain, Jonathan Winters learned to joke and make others laugh.

Tracie's parents divorced one year ago. Tracie has problems accepting her own feelings: "Sometimes my attitude is not good. I get so angry at my father when I know I shouldn't worry about what he is doing. Sometimes I say that I hate my mom when I don't want to do something like clean my room or wash the dog. I don't really hate her; I'm just upset with myself."

Kara, who's thirteen, says that she needs to change her temper. She has been through many stepfathers, but it is her mother's use of alcohol that makes her most angry. "I've developed a temper because I've had to defend myself around my mother's alcohol," she writes. "If I could change one thing about my parents, I'd tell them, 'No alcohol'! Divorce causes hate and torn lives. It *always* hurts the child most, and I can't name one person that *likes* it!"

Sierra writes that she wants to change her "feelings toward the way everything has happened. The worst thing about divorce is having one parent leave and move away. I'd tell adults not to ever get married if they have any doubts that their marriage is going to make it."

HOW HAS DIVORCE CHANGED YOU?

Do you think your parents' breakup has changed your personality? Do you feel worthless? empty? ignored?

Researchers have noticed that teenagers often react to divorce in harmful ways. Girls often tend to begin to use drugs and/or alcohol, and boys may drift toward drugs and crime.[3] Why? Maybe some kids begin to practice these destructive behaviors because they simply don't care much about themselves anymore.

Susan Grobman, a high school junior, writes that divorce changed her greatly:

> Until the divorce my feelings were limited to my own self-doubt and guilt. After the divorce my fears took on a much greater scope. I became a classic worrier. Every problem seemed dramatic and ominous, such as the time when my father took all of my mother's credit cards away. I knew at that moment my life would be different from all my friends.[4]

IF YOU BEGIN TO SLIP

If you experience an emotional upheaval during your parents' divorce, you are *completely normal*. No one expects you to remain perfectly in control of yourself when your life is changing so dramatically.

You may find that as hard as you try to study, you simply can't do your best on tests. Or maybe studying is the only thing you want to do because if you're thinking about schoolwork, you can't think about the problems at home! Your emotions will fluctuate as you adjust in different ways, so try to accept and understand yourself.

If your grades are falling at school or if you simply want to find someone to talk to, make an appointment with your guidance counselor. Think of your counselor as a "life coach." He or she has talked to others who are in your situation, so nothing you say will surprise the counselor very much. Your counselor can help you examine your feelings as well as get you back on the academic track.

You may not feel like doing much of anything in the first few weeks after one of your parents leaves, but there will come a time when you will be able to get out of your depressed mood and enjoy life once again. When that time comes, take responsibility for your life and get out there and make something good of it! Just because your parents had a problem they couldn't resolve doesn't mean that you are doomed to failure. Your life can be different. You can make that choice now.

If, however, you have been depressed for months and you can't seem to get over your feelings, you probably need to talk to a counselor. There is within each of us a protective mechanism that covers our hurts through denial or depression, and if you have been hurt so badly that you are still covered up inside, it may be time to reach out for help.

TALK, TALK, TALK!

Have you ever had a splinter that you couldn't get out from under your skin? Even a tiny splinter in a finger or toe can cause horrible pain, and the longer it remains, the more it hurts! Soon your entire body throbs with pain, and the area around the tiny intruder turns red with rage. Ouch!

Hidden feelings are "emotional splinters." Until you are willing to talk about your real feelings—those feelings hidden deep down inside—they will continue to cause you pain. You may think if you don't talk about them they will go away, but they won't. They will remain inside and fester for years to come. You have to talk about them and bring them out into the open in order to let them heal.

Find someone you trust—a Christian school counselor, a pastor, your youth leader—and let him or her help you examine and understand your feelings. The person you choose to confide in should be someone who really cares about you and respects your feelings and privacy. Be careful whom you choose.

DON'T LET ANYONE TAKE ADVANTAGE OF YOU

When you are hurt, you are vulnerable, and there are people who would like to take advantage of your vulnerability. There are men and older boys who would take advantage of a floundering girl and involve her in a sexual relationship. There are friends who would like to involve you in their reckless activities—drugs, drinking, and sex.

You may want acceptance and security so badly that you will give into this pressure. But remember—if people can't accept you as you are, right now, they are not accepting you at all!

My husband and I were worried when Tammy's parents divorced. Tammy was a very pretty and mature-looking young girl who immediately took up with a nineteen-year-old boy. His parents had recently divorced, too, and Tammy said they "needed each other." They certainly did need someone, but we weren't sure they needed each other! They didn't have the maturity to help each other. Both were hurting and confused; neither had any answers.

It is natural that you should go "looking for love" after your parents divorce. You may think you have found love in a certain young man or woman, but "romantic love" is not really what you need at this point.

School guidance counselors tell us that each year there are a number of girls who go looking for love and end up pregnant. Many of these girls honestly don't know how they got pregnant. It's hard to believe that in this sexually open society this could happen, but it does.

If you don't know all you'd like to know about sex, ask your parents, your youth pastor, or your counselor to talk it over with you or refer you to a good book. (Jim Watkins's book *Sex Is Not a Four-Letter Word* should tell you everything you need to know about sex and dating.) It's important for you to know what sex is, when it is appropriate, and God's purpose for it. Most of all, you need to know you don't have to have sex with anyone to find love. There are people who love you just as you are right now. You should never have to earn or pay for love.

If you have been or are being molested, never, ever feel that the attention you receive from this person is worth the bad feelings the activity causes you. "Bad love" is not better than no love at all. You are not receiving love from a molester—you are simply being used to satisfy his selfish desires. Child molestation is a crime. It is not right to touch another person in his or her private places, and if anyone is asking or forcing you to participate in this activity, you should find someone who can make them stop!

"I want to tell kids that if an adult wants everything to be secretive, real hush-hush, kids should tell someone they trust—an adult who can put a stop to what's going on," says Garrett Gilbert, who was molested several times by two adult men who were friends of her family. "If you let fear stop you from telling, you will only hurt yourself."[5]

Run today to someone who can help you. Call a counselor, a pastor, or the police. You have the right to say no.

SEARCH FOR "FAMILY LOVE"

What can ease the pain you feel? Look for family love. You can find this kind of love in your church and in the Christian homes of your friends. Find homes that are stable and open, and if you're invited to go over or join a family outing, go!

Don't forget you can still find family love within your own family. Your parents have not lost their love for you; you are still their child, and they love you deeply.

You can also find family love within God's family of Christian brothers and sisters. Read Ephesians 4:14-21, and you'll see that Paul asked that God's entire family be strengthened with love and power. Paul noted that God's family members have access to the immeasurable love of Christ.

YOU ARE LOVABLE

You are lovable just as you are. God created you for a purpose. Of course we all have room for improvement in our appearance and in our character, but to love yourself as God loves you, you need to accept the things that you cannot change.

What are some things you can't change? Your biological parents, your race, your sex, your birth order, your brothers and sisters, your mental abilities, certain physical features, and your age. Pretty much anything else about yourself that you consider "defective" can be changed.

What is it you don't like about yourself? Your weight? Your height? Your nose? Improve yourself if you can, and accept the things you can't improve. Lots of young people spend hours and loads of money trying to look like an airbrushed picture of a model, but why should you waste your time trying to look like someone else? Standards of beauty change from season to season, but ideals of inner beauty are changeless. Our ideal should be to be like Christ.

Our outward features are only the frame on the picture. The picture is your inner self, and it's usually revealed through your facial expression, or countenance. We've all seen striking girls and handsome guys with hard, stony, unattractive expressions. We've also seen young people who didn't measure up to perfect physical standards but were good-looking because their countenance shone with the joy of the Lord and the peace that comes from knowing Christ.

GOD THINKS YOU'RE SPECIAL

If you've been struggling with feelings of worthlessness, perhaps you've forgotten what makes a person truly valuable. It's not beauty or brains that makes us creatures of worth, it's the fact that God created us and loves us. As Christians we have the Holy Spirit living inside us; we are *something special!* God knew you were a unique person even before you were born: "Before I was born the Lord called me; from my birth he has made mention of my name" (Isaiah 49:1).

If you feel inferior because you don't have a dad, God even promises to be a "father to the fatherless" (Psalm 68:5). Because you can trust God to pull you and your family through difficult days ahead, you can also trust him for the way he designed you! The Bible says that "we are God's workmanship." The psalmist wrote:

> For you created my inmost being; you knit me together in my mother's womb. I praise you because I am fearfully and wonderfully made; your works are wonderful, I know that full well.
>
> My frame was not hidden from you when I was made in

the secret place. When I was woven together in the depths of the earth, your eyes saw my unformed body. All the days ordained for me were written in your book before one of them came to be. (Psalm 139:13-16)

God not only chose who you were to be and what you were to look like, he chose the mother and father who brought you into the world. You were not a mistake! God also chose all the factors and circumstances in your parents' lives that surrounded your conception and birth.

Even if you are not growing up with your biological parents, you can be sure that the parent or guardians who care for you are the right ones for you. God chose Amram and Jochebed to bring Moses into the world and to give him his early training, but then God chose Pharaoh's daughter to give Moses special training in the royal courts of Egypt (read about it in Exodus 2:1-10). God chose Elkanah and Hannah to be the parents of Samuel; however, through circumstances beyond Samuel's control, he was raised by Eli in the tabernacle.

"God has a special purpose for each of our lives," says Bill Gothard. "If he allows me to be brought up by only one parent or by those other than my parents, I can be confident that he has an extra-special purpose for my life."[6]

If God in his wisdom has somehow removed you from one or both of your biological parents, can you honestly thank him for doing so? I was a little surprised that several of the young people I interviewed for this book expressed relief that they were no longer living with either parent. In one situation, sexual abuse had alienated the father and destroyed the mother. The young girl was happier living with another relative.

How can you be happy when your parents are constantly fighting and bickering over child-support payments and visitation schedules? This may be your motivation to learn what *not* to do if you want to have a successful marriage. This bad situation may encourage you to grow closer to the Lord in prayer and reading the Bible. God can be your Father, and being his child can develop in you inner qualities of peace, patience, and self-control.

So no matter how divorce changes you, let it be for your good. God loves you, he has made you the way you are, and you are wonderful! He will guide you and take care of your family.

FOR MEMORIZATION AND MEDITATION

Psalm 139:13-16

"For you created my inmost being; you knit me together in my mother's womb. I praise you because I am fearfully and wonderfully made; your works are wonderful, I know that full well. My frame was not hidden from you when I was made in the secret place. When I was woven together in the depths of the earth, your eyes saw my unformed body. All the days ordained for me were written in your book before one of them came to be."

Broken China, Healing Hearts

I know we were luckier than a lot of people. When we crawled out of the bathroom the next morning, we found that our house had only lost part of its roof and a couple of windows. Everything was wet, of course, and nothing electrical worked—but we were alive. God had answered my prayer to save us, and I didn't care about the mess. I was just grateful to be in one piece.

"What a dump," Kenyon said dully as we picked our way through the debris on the floor.

Mom didn't say anything. She just walked zombielike into the kitchen as if she were on her way to fix breakfast. She walked through the kitchen and paused in the dining room, then Kenyon and I heard an earsplitting wail. "The china!" she cried. "It's all broken. Your grandmother's china."

Mom sank into a heap on the wet floor, and Kenyon and I came and stood behind her. The plywood Dad had placed over the dining room window had been ripped away, and now nothing remained but a gaping hole in the wall. The hole had let the winds in, and the intruding force had literally toppled Mom's china hutch. Little shards of green and yellow china lay all over the floor among piles of splintered wood. Several sharp pieces of glass and wood were even embedded in the wall.

Kenyon surveyed the damage and gave a low whistle. "Guess it's a good thing we were moving, huh?" he quipped, trying to smile. "Come on, Kels, let's go check on our rooms."

I didn't want to leave Mom, but I didn't know what to say or do. I didn't care about the china. All that mattered was that we were alive and well.

I patted Mom on the shoulder, and she stopped crying long enough to grab my hand. "Thanks, Kelsey," she said, looking up at me through her tears. She smiled a little quivery smile. "I guess we've just got to do a little cleaning up and then move on, right?"

I nodded. "That's right, Mom," I answered. "We'll be OK. I've been praying a lot lately, and I think God will help us through *everything*."

Mom stood up and brushed off her jeans. "Yes, I believe you're right," she agreed, her voice firmer now. "I guess we won't be moving, huh? Who's going to buy a house with only half a roof?"

Mom sighed and looked around, then she slipped an arm around my shoulder. "You're right, Kelsey," she said, giving me a gentle squeeze. "Things around here might be messy for a while, but we're going to be just fine."

ACCEPTING THE FACTS

Unless you were a victim of child abuse or the child of an alcoholic, you probably liked your family the way it was before the divorce. Sure, there were bad days, but there were good days, too. There were magical times when everyone managed to coast along without any major eruptions; there were hilarious times of family togetherness.

You probably didn't see the private arguments and talks your parents had about their problems. If they were like many parents, they tried to put on a good front for their kids. When they divorced, it's almost a sure bet that at some point you wished—maybe even prayed—that your parents would get back together.

For some kids that wish comes true. Some parents are able to work out their problems, and the families reunite and are stronger as a result of their trouble. But the sad fact is that most parents don't get back together.

Divorce is really hard when one of your parents is still hoping, wishing, and praying that the other will come home. Tom was miserable for nearly two years while he and Becky lived apart before she finally filed for divorce. Tom tried changing his job, his appearance, his clothes, and even his personality—anything to make Becky love him again. But the marriage was over. Becky wanted to leave her old life behind and begin a new one.

Their daughter, Tabitha, didn't know if her family would be back together or not. Tom kept telling her to pray that God would bring her mom back, but her mother just shook her head and said, "No way, honey." It was difficult. Tabitha wanted to believe that God would answer her prayers, and when the divorce was final, Tabitha felt that God had betrayed her. They were a Christian family, so how could such a thing happen to them?

WONDERFUL ISN'T GUARANTEED

God doesn't force people, even Christian people, to do his will. We are created with a free will, and we are free to choose whether we will serve or reject Christ. We can choose to follow or not to follow his will for our life. We can choose to do our own thing anywhere along the way. Life is a series of choices, of actions and reactions, and because we have a free will, we don't always choose God's perfect will.

We also live in a sinful world. Do you ever wonder why there are earthquakes and wars and sickness and painful, tragic deaths? Does almighty God sit up in heaven on a throne and arrange these awful things according to his whims and wishes? Did he plan a divorce, two inches of growth, a strict teacher, and exactly forty-two pimples for you this year simply because he felt like it?

I don't think so. God allows things, good and bad, to happen so that we can be made into the image of Christ. Our purpose in life as Christians is to glorify God and honor him, no matter what we do. A man who is a preacher is no more important to God than a man who is a street sweeper. And the street sweeper who is humble and Christlike is more in God's will than a preacher who preaches for the wrong reasons.

Since the world we live in is filled with sin and actually managed by Satan, it is no wonder that we are surrounded by evil situations. Everywhere you look you see people who are pursuing personal pleasure and profit at the expense of their families and others. Perhaps one of these things ultimately led to the breakup of your parents' marriage.

ACTIONS AND REACTIONS

Although God cares a lot about our actions in life, maybe he cares even more about our *reactions*. Is it of great eternal significance whether or not a baseball player hits a home run on a given day? Isn't God more interested in how that baseball player *reacts* to either hitting the home run or striking out? God cares more about a person's character than his abilities.

How did you react to your family's divorce? Were you angry? bitter? sad? relieved? There's nothing you can do about the *action* (the divorce); it is your parents' doing, and you should not feel responsible for it. But you are responsible for your *reaction* to it.

Of course you will grieve. Of course you will be confused and hurt. Of course you'd like to see them back together. There may be months when you feel like belting anyone who would dare to tell you to "keep your chin up and keep going." That's OK.

It will take time for you to get used to the reality that your parents have divorced and that reconciliation is out of the question. It will take time to become accustomed to living with only one parent and visiting another. It will take time to adjust to the idea of your parents dating other people. If one of your parents remarries, it will take time to learn to live with a new stepparent.

Take the time you need to work through these changes (a few weeks or months, not an eternity), and then set out to grow again. Remember, it is your reactions that really matter. God cares about your *character.*

What do you get when you squeeze an orange? Orange juice. You get *whatever is inside.* When the pressure is on and you find yourself being squeezed on all sides, whatever is inside you will come out. If you have filled yourself with positive attitudes and good reactions to your situations, then goodness will spill out on those around you. On the other hand, if you have sulked, grown bitter, hateful, or resentful, nothing but bitterness, hate, and resentment will pour out.

You probably learned in science that for every action, there is an equal and opposite reaction. That's true. And no matter what your parents have decided about reconciliation, may your *reactions* be honoring to the Lord.

MOVING AHEAD

You've faced some serious obstacles in your life. Some kids will never have to face the problems you have, and sometimes you wonder if life is fair.

You could spend most of your time dwelling on the past, but if you want to be successful and have the fulfilling life God intends for you, you'll have to get up and move on.

Proverbs 3:6 tells us, "In all your ways acknowledge him, and he will make your paths straight." Paths are made for walking! And if the path leads over a rocky, troublesome mountain, well, remember—it's the *bumps* that you climb on!

Did you know that the eagle's only obstacle to flying higher, faster, and farther is the air? But if you removed the air and placed the bird in a vacuum, it couldn't fly at all! The very element that causes the resistance to flying is the one necessary for flight.

In the same way, the main obstacle that a power boat must overcome is the water against the propeller. Yet if it were not for this resistance, the boat could not move at all. Zig Ziglar says it well:

> Obstacles wake us up and lead us to our abilities. Exertion gives us new power, so out of our difficulties new strength is born. Out of an obstacle comes strength; out of disappointment comes growth; out of deprivation comes desire.[1]

CHOOSE YOUR FUTURE

Twin boys grew up in a home where the father was an alcoholic who couldn't hold a job and spent most of his time down at the local bar. When he was home, he beat his wife and ended up divorcing her.

One of the twins married early. He didn't go to college, couldn't hold a job, and spent most of his time down at the local bar. When he was home, he beat his wife and ended up divorcing her.

The other boy went to college and took his time getting married. He had a lovely wife, a successful career, and raised beautiful, happy children.

Later in life both brothers were asked why they became what they were. Both gave the same answer: "Because of my father."[2]

What happened? Out of the same experience came both depression and determination. Each boy made his own choice. Which choice will you make?

FORGIVENESS IS THE KEY

One step that's crucial in moving on after a divorce is deciding to forgive your parents for the hurts they may have caused you. If you decide that you cannot forgive someone, you practically guarantee that you will become like the person you hate. You may not do the things he does, but your negative attitude will mirror the attitude of the person you cannot forgive.

Our attitudes determine our actions; therefore, attitudes are very important. If your father drinks and beats you and your mom, you learn to hate him for his actions. As a child you may not understand that his *attitudes* are responsible for his actions—he is selfish, proud, and cruel.

If you cannot forgive him, you will dwell on his actions and review them often in your mind. The more you think about him, the deeper your bitterness and dislike will grow. Finally, one day you will marry, and, although you may not be an alcoholic or a child-beater, your inability to forgive your father will bring the same attitudes you hated into your life. Without realizing it, you will become just like him—selfish, proud, and cruel.

When you forgive, though, your attitudes and actions reflect those of Christ, who was loving, forgiving, and selfless. You will be able to see that the things your parents did were the result of sin and confusion. When you forgive your parents, you keep the door open for a good relationship. If you cannot forgive, you close the door and alienate your parents forever.

If one or both or your parents don't know Christ, forgiving them for any offenses they have committed against you is so important. If you have reacted wrongly to them, ask for their forgiveness.

Your actions will show Christ's love and forgiveness and may be instrumental in bringing your parents to salvation in Christ.

There is nothing you or your parents have done that is beyond forgiveness. In 1 John 1:9 we read, "If we confess our sins, he is faithful and just and will forgive us our sins and purify us from all unrighteousness."

Kathy once told me about her mother. "I hate her," she said bluntly. "She's an alcoholic, and when I have to visit her, she is just awful. I can never forgive her. Never."

Kathy was not a happy girl, and her bitterness showed on her face. But slowly, over a period of time, Kathy began to learn from the Bible about the importance of forgiveness. One day she came up to me, and her eyes danced with delight. "I can forgive my mother. I still get angry with her sometimes, but I wrote her a letter and told her I forgive her. I feel like a new person!"

If you can forgive others and allow Christ to heal the hurts of your heart, you will be on your way to *growing* through the painful experience of divorce.

WHAT ABOUT YOU?

Perhaps you've never allowed Christ to come into your life and offer *you* his forgiveness. Jesus knows us better than anyone else ever could. He even knows the ugly things we keep hidden from the rest of the world, yet he wants to be our best friend!

Even though our sin "divorced" us from his holy presence, he still loves us and wants us to love him. His love is complete and perfect (not something that you "fall into" or "fall out of"), and he gave us the very best he had to offer, his life. Christ loved you enough to take on all the sins you have committed or ever will commit, and he paid the penalty for those sins by dying on the cross. He didn't want to die. But he did it for you. His commitment to love was that strong!

Love really should be based on commitment, but as you know, adults often find they simply don't have what it takes to be true to that commitment. But *Jesus will never fail you.* Have you committed your life to him? If you haven't, would you like to do so right now?

Those who have committed their lives to Christ are his children. God is a father to the fatherless and a friend always. He can see you through any trial. His love and the wisdom contained in his Word, the Bible, can make you strong to face your problems. Trust him!

EPILOGUE

To Sum It All Up

Bet you didn't know reading my ninth-grade journal would be like this, did you, Miss Westgate? Things were really rough after the hurricane and the divorce. We all had days when we cried in frustration and helplessness—even Kenyon finally broke down and cried one night. I think it was harder for him because somehow he had the idea that boys aren't supposed to cry.

But my youth pastor at church helped us a lot, and we helped each other. Mom's doing fine in her new job, Dad's got a new girlfriend (so long, Alanna Dansk!), and Kenyon's going out for track. With his long legs, he'll be a star—you wait and see.

But the one who helped me the most was Jesus Christ. I don't know how you feel about God, Miss Westgate, but I couldn't have pulled through all this without him. I don't feel so embarrassed about my family anymore, and I know I'm not alone. Jesus has been with me every step of the way. And the family I have—Mom and Kenyon in one house, and Dad in his apartment—they all love me, and I love them. This whole mess hasn't been easy, but Mom was right—we're going to be just fine.

FOR MEMORIZATION AND MEDITATION

Mark 11:25

"And when you stand praying, if you hold anything against anyone, forgive him, so that your Father in heaven may forgive you your sins."

Luke 17:3-4

"If your brother sins, rebuke him, and if he repents, forgive him. If he sins against you seven times in a day, and seven times comes back to you and says, 'I repent,' forgive him."

Ephesians 4:32

"Be kind and compassionate to one another, forgiving each other, just as in Christ God forgave you."

Colossians 3:13

"Bear with each other and forgive whatever grievances you may have against one another. Forgive as the Lord forgave you."

NO SUCH THING AS DIVORCE

by Bob Bennett

Oh my dear children
How I love you with my life
And that will never change
Though your mom is not my wife
It's true I promised you
That this would never come to be
Please forgive me

118

When people fall in love
They never see the day
When one will ask the other
To pack up and move away
And I know that I have told you
I am sorry for my part
There's nothing I can do now
But to tell you from my heart

There is no such thing as divorce
Between a father and his son
Between a daddy and his daughter
There's no such thing as divorce
No matter what has happened
No matter what will be
There's no power that can make us anything but family
There is no such thing as divorce between you and me

I know that sometimes
You are worried I will go
And at first I felt like running
But now you need to know
That when I looked down deep inside me
It did not take long to see
That, little ones, you are
The most important thing to me

Sometimes I cry over
The things I can't undo
And the words I never
Should have said in front of you
But I pray the good
Will somehow overcome the bad

And where I failed as a husband
I'll succeed as your dad

Oh my dear children
As you grow so I will pray
That I will always listen
To the things you'll need to say
For I will always be your daddy
I will answer when you call
And I will ask the Lord of heaven
To be a Father to us all

N O T E S

CHAPTER T W O . *The Dark Blue Volvo*

1. Anne Claire and H. S. Vigeveno, *No One Gets Divorced Alone* (Ventura, Calif.: Regal Books, 1987), 75.
2. "The Adult Children Also Suffer the Effects of Parental Divorce," *Lynchburg News and Daily Advance*, 27 November 1983.

CHAPTER T H R E E . *My Love Letter*

1. "Young Children of Divorce: Depressed, Wary, Subdued," *USA Today*, September 1987, 10.
2. Kathy Callahan-Howell, "Helping Children Cope with Divorce," *Parents and Children* (Wheaton, Ill.: Victor Books, 1986), 682.

CHAPTER F O U R . *The Neon Rose*

1. Susan Grobman, "Child of Divorce," *USA Today*, July 1987, 41.

CHAPTER F I V E . *House for Sale*

1. "No-Fault Divorce an Economic Disaster for Wives, Children," *U.S. News and World Report*, 4 November 1985, 63.
2. "Never a Right Age," *Scientific American* (September 1987): 32.
3. Benjamin Carson, telephone conversation with author, 10 July 1989.

CHAPTER S I X . *Alanna Dansk*

1. Jeff Meer, "Divorce: Do It for the Kids?" *Psychology Today*, July 1987, 21.

CHAPTER E I G H T . *The Ugly, Muddy Hole*

1. Clifton Fadiman, ed., *The Little, Brown Book of Anecdotes* (Boston: Little, Brown and Company, 1985), 540.

CHAPTER N I N E . *Storm Alert*

1. Zig Ziglar, *Raising Positive Kids in a Negative World* (Nashville: Thomas Nelson Publishers, 1985), 158.
2. James Dobson, *Hide or Seek* (Old Tappan, N.J.: Fleming H. Revell Company, 1979), 158.
3. Jennett Conant with Pat Wingert, "You'd Better Sit Down, Kids," *Newsweek*, 24 August 1987, 58.
4. Grobman, "Child of Divorce," 41.
5. Garrett Gilbert as told to Carol Elrod, "A Victim Speaks Out," *Woman's Day*, 15 April 1986, 113.
6. Bill Gothard, *Self-Acceptance* (Oak Brook, Ill.: Institute in Basic Youth Conflicts, 1985), 4.

CHAPTER T E N . *Broken China, Healing Hearts*

1. Ziglar, *Raising Positive Kids*, 37.
2. Ronald P. Hutchcraft, "Life as a Single Parent," *Parents and Teenagers* (Wheaton, Ill.: Victor Books, 1984), 472.

Printed in the United States
21514LVS00001B/118